FRAGMENTS FROM
A FRACTURED MIND

Short Fiction and Nonfiction

Richard Davidson

RADMAR Publishing Group

RADMAR

This anthology is dedicated to the members of my Critique Group who inspire my writing in many ways.

CONTENTS

PART ONE – FICTION AND POETRY

BEYOND THE EULOGY

He turned left, only to see a wall twelve feet in front of him. At first he thought it was a dead end, but a patch of light on the left wall of the corridor suggested a side branch opening to the right, just before the blocking wall. He turned into that narrower hallway and saw that the room numbers were unconventional, counting upward on the left set of doors and downward on the doors to his right. *How could such an esteemed institution as Terwillegar University be so disorganized?* As he walked down the side corridor, he noticed that the floor sloped downhill, ending at a cross-corridor extending to both the left and the right. *They must have connected two buildings that were built separately and not meant to be joined.* His direction sheet indicated that he was in the School of Social Sciences. The place was unusual, but not at all social. He hadn't encountered a single individual in the hallways. He thought his destination, Room 367 ½ was a mistake, but in a building as complex as this, it might be considered normal.

Normal or not, he couldn't find the bizarre room number. He finally gave up and knocked on the door of Room 367. The shouted response was, "Don't stand on ceremony. Come in so we can get started."

He donned a pair of wire-framed spectacles. As he did so, he appeared to lose height and become younger. Then he opened the door to reveal a classroom where a small group of students and an instructor awaited him. He turned to the instructor and said, "Excuse me; I'm lost. I'm looking for Room 367 ½, but I can't find it. Does it exist, or am I supposed to be here?"

The instructor responded, "You're supposed to be here, because without you, we don't have the required fifteen students for me to teach this adult education course. What's your last name?"

"It's Einstein, but I'm not here to take a course. I'm from *People* Magazine. They promised me a promotion if I get an interview with Professor Ignatius M. Hardaway. He's listed as having his office in Room 367 ½."

"Glad to meet you, Einstein. Professor Hardaway never gives interviews, and you won't find that unusual office number. Stay, and take this course. I need one more student registered, or these other fourteen students lose their credits, and I don't get paid. My name's Frank Babylon."

"I'm not a student, and I don't even know the name of your course."

"The course is Eulogy Structure. With a name like Einstein, you shouldn't have any difficulty handling it."

"I'm Julius Einstein, not Genius Einstein. I'm not an academic. I'll lose my opportunity at *People* Magazine if I don't get an interview with Professor Hardaway."

Babylon stared at the wall thoughtfully, as though he was debating with himself. He said, "I'll make a deal with you. Professor Hardaway was my doctoral thesis adviser. If you take and complete this course, I'll set you up for an interview with him."

Julius extended his hand for an agreement handshake. "You have a deal, Frank. I'll do it if I can stall my boss and get her to extend my deadline for the interview."

Frank Babylon asked, "Are you somewhere in Albert Einstein's family tree?"

"I'm down in some remote corner of it."

"Then you're the result of relativity."

"You're not much of a comedian. I can't even count the number of Albert Einstein and relativity jokes I've suffered in my lifetime. How about you? Have you received many Babylon, or should I say, babble-on, jokes?"

"More than a few, Einstein." Babylon turned toward the other students. "We now have enough people to make this an official course. Time is too short for a lesson this period. We'll start studying eulogies next time."

As Frank Babylon shuffled his notes prior to the second session, Einstein approached and caught his attention. "My editor won't extend my deadline until the end of the semester. Can we rework our agreement so I get my interview after a few weeks and then complete your course afterward?"

"Einstein, we have a deal, and you'll have to stick with it. No changes. Now, sit down so I can get started."

Babylon scanned his students and took them to be a motley assortment. "We'll begin with voluntary introductions. State your first name, a few words about your background, and your reason for taking this course. Who'll start? Einstein? No need to stand when you speak."

Einstein said, "I didn't want to take this course."

A soft voice broke the silence.

"My name is Patricia. I've returned to college after a ten year break. My soldier husband died in Iraq. I want to teach history and this course is a requirement."

Einstein opened an ornately bound pocket notebook and wrote in old-fashioned script: *Greater love hath no man ...*

Babylon said, "Next."

"I'm Barry. I'm an actor, so I expect I'll miss a few classes because of auditions. I'm here because I learned that you don't give final exams."

Several people murmured.

Einstein wrote: *This man began to build and was not able to finish.*

Babylon nodded. "Barry's correct. No final exam in this course. I decide whether you pass or fail, so pay attention and try to learn something."

An older man waved. "I'm Myron. My doctor says that I have less than a year to live. I'm here to learn how to write my own eulogy. No one fully appreciated me during my lifetime, so I want to leave them with a tribute that tells them what they missed."

Babylon sympathized, "Sorry to hear about your one year outlook, Myron."

Myron shrugged his shoulders. "C'est la vie."

Einstein wrote: *The last shall be first.*

A pregnant young woman gestured for attention. "My name is Felicity. I work at an animal cemetery. I get paid extra if I write eulogies for departed pets. I'm hoping this class will help me spice them up."

Einstein wrote: *His eye is on the sparrow.*

The next person said, "I'm Mary, and I'm here to get an easy credit. I don't expect to have anything to do with eulogies after this course."

"Very honest of you, Mary. I have no problem with that."

Einstein wrote: *If a man will not work, he shall not eat.*

Wally, Herman, Gina, Jose, Bella, and John each echoed Mary, saying they were there for an easy credit. John added that he wasn't quite sure what a eulogy was.

"Trudy here. I work for a funeral home, and I'm going to be writing life highlights pieces for clients to be orally presented and printed in the funeral service programs. Those are eulogies, John."

John gave a thumbs-up gesture.

Einstein wrote: *Ashes to ashes.*

A middle-aged man in well worn work clothes stood even though Babylon had said it wasn't required. "I'll be next. Call me Gus. I work for St. Emily's Shelter for the Homeless. Most people don't realize that many homeless folks had normal and important life stories before they landed on the streets. I'm going to write send-off pieces telling the world how valuable its deceased homeless sons and daughters were. St. Emily's is asking the Chicago *Sun-Times* to print them."

Einstein wrote: *Blessed are the poor in spirit, for theirs is the kingdom of heaven.*

An older woman hesitated. Then she said, "I'm Martha. Myron said that he wanted to write a eulogy for himself that would make folks appreciate his life achievements. I want to do the same for my grandson, Paul. He died in a highway shooting and flaming car crash last week. He was only eighteen and had all sorts of potential for the future. The memorial service is in three weeks. I hope I'll learn enough by that time to do him justice."

All conversations stopped as Martha wiped tears

from her eyes.

Einstein wrote: *Lazarus.*

Babylon noted as he prepared to start the third class that a few seats were empty. Wally, Bella, Jose, John, and Barry had not made it to the session. They were all in the 'easy credit' group per the introductions, except for Barry, the actor. He wondered whether those individuals would be back or if they had dropped out of the course. No matter; the rule at Terwillegar University was that fifteen students were required to start teaching a course, but fees weren't refundable, so there was no minimum number for those completing the course.

Babylon quieted the chatter. "We have a few empty seats today, so I'll sit with you."

Patricia raised her hand. "Should we take notes, or will you give us handouts?"

"Take notes or not as you wish, but I'll expect you to discuss the subject matter later. You don't need to raise your hand to speak. Jump into the discussion whenever the current speaker pauses. Just don't interrupt anyone mid-sentence."

Babylon noticed several pads of paper emerging from backpacks. Einstein already had his reporter's notebook out.

"We're going to start with eulogies in history before we talk about creating one. In the past, these speeches were much longer than is acceptable today. That doesn't mean that they were any better; only that they were formal and detailed. One reason for this was the lack of mass communication. Someone giving a eulogy included background information in case listeners were unfamiliar with the deceased person. By the way, historically, almost all eulogies were delivered by male speakers."

Felicity said, "I can't believe that. Frontier women had to say some words over their husbands' graves."

Babylon nodded. "Good point. Remember that I said 'almost all'. The first historic eulogy we're going to discuss is one for George Washington that was delivered by Henry Lee, a major general in the Continental Army."

Einstein interrupted. "From a relativity standpoint, was Henry Lee related to General Robert E. Lee of Civil War fame?"

"I don't know, but I get your point, Einstein. I won't bother you with any more relativity jokes. Continuing with Lee's eulogy for George Washington, it was so well received that Lee reprinted and sold it as a fifteen page brochure. Today, memorial speeches are typically two to four typewritten pages."

Martha said, "That's a relief. I don't read all that well, and I wouldn't want to struggle through reading fifteen pages to honor my grandson. If I could get by with writing two or three pages about Paul, I'd be able to add more without notes."

Myron said, "It would really be a kick if I did such a good job eulogizing myself that someone would want to reprint the speech and sell it."

Most of the class laughed. Patricia patted Myron's shoulder.

Babylon continued. "Henry Lee's eulogy was long and full of resume details about George Washington, but nowadays, few people remember more than one key nugget from it."

Mary sat straighter, suddenly interested. "What's still remembered?"

First in war, first in peace, and first in the hearts of his countrymen, he was second to none in humble and enduring scenes of private life.

Einstein nodded. "I remember reading the first half of that quotation." About Washington, he wrote: *He took ... seed of the land and planted it in fertile soil.*

Babylon said, "If you want to read other eulogies for George Washington, along with Henry Lee's complete speech, browse the books and reprints on my desk. Look them over for the rest of the period. You may leave at any point after examining them. Next time, we'll discuss Lincoln eulogies."

When the fourth session started, Frank Babylon looked around the room and then walked to the door, scanning the hallway in both directions. He couldn't believe how rapidly he was losing students. Attendance had diminished to Patricia, Felicity, Gus, and Einstein – only four students. This was getting a bit ridiculous.

"Do any of you know where the others are? Do you see them outside of class?"

Babylon received head shakes in response from Patricia, Felicity, and Gus. Einstein looked placid as he wrote something in his notebook.

"We'll start discussing Lincoln eulogies. Perhaps more folks will arrive during the session.

"John Wilkes Booth shot Abraham Lincoln at Ford's Theatre in Washington, DC, while Lincoln and his wife were attending a performance of *Our American Cousin.*"

The students leaned forward, intrigued by the assassination story.

"President Lincoln was shot on the evening of April 14, 1865. He died the following morning, April 15, and the eulogy we'll study was given on April 19 by Rev. Edward E. Cutter. As was the case with the Henry Lee eulogy for George Washington, Cutter's Lincoln eulogy is very long. Of special significance is its start.

On the 19th of April, 1775, the first blood of the Revolution was shed at Lexington.

On the 19th of April, 1861, the first blood of this terrible conflict between freedom and slavery was shed in Baltimore.

On this 19th of April, 1865, Abraham Lincoln, the first President of these United States whose name and administration will be forever associated with Universal Emancipation, struck down by the assassin's hand, is carried to his burial at Washington; and a nation is in tears.

Babylon continued, "The three similar dates are significant, both because of their historic impact and because twenty years later, a safe was found containing some of Lincoln's personal papers and treasures. Its combination was set at 4-19-15. The safe dial knob had fifty positions, so fifteen with the full turn of fifty before it was the same as sixty-five."

Gus stood. "Are you saying that President Lincoln knew when he was going to be eulogized in setting that combination?"

"Not quite, Gus; anyone could have locked those items into that safe after Lincoln's death. It's an unanswerable question."

Einstein interrupted. "You're not suggesting the repetitions of the April nineteenth dates in that eulogy were a secret message, are you?"

Babylon answered defensively, "They could have been. Widely circulated speeches, especially during war years, have been known to include coded information. The full text of Cutter's Lincoln eulogy is on my desk.

Examine it to discover whether other repetitions or word patterns might contain hidden messages. Next time, I'll show you a template and principles for writing a eulogy."

Einstein wrote about Lincoln: *Even though I walk through the valley of the shadow of death ...*

When Frank Babylon walked into his classroom for his fifth session, he saw only Julius Einstein there, sitting on the corner of Frank's desk.

"Where is everyone, Einstein?"

"Everyone is me. Since I'm not a real student, you have no remaining students, and the course is at its end. I'm the only person who stayed for your entire course, so my part of the bargain is done. I want my interview with Professor Hardaway."

Babylon raised a questioning eyebrow. "I smell some mischief here. Did you take the other students away from my course?"

"Let's just say I streamlined and improved your course. I couldn't get my editor to delay my deadline until the end of your semester, so I arranged to shorten the course."

"What do you mean?"

"The others didn't drop out. I paid Barry, the actor, to give them lessons in another room, using guidelines I supplied. While you've been reviewing famous eulogies in history, Barry has given them hands-on lessons in writing and delivering their own memorial speeches. He even showed them tricks to keep from crying as they delivered their eulogies."

"I was going to get to that later."

"Babylon, later is now, and you had better give them all passing grades. Every student has written at least one eulogy and presented it in front of the others for critique feedback. They all understand how to do it. If you wish, I'll take you to that room so that you can sit in on the process."

"That won't be necessary. They all pass. I'll sign my grade sheet now." Babylon dropped his pen on the desk after signing. "I give up, Julius. You do have some of that Einstein blood in your veins."

"Fine. Now show me the office or cubbyhole called Room 367 ½ so that I can interview Professor Hardaway."

Babylon went to his desk and removed a key from his top left drawer. He inserted the key into the lock on a small door in the rear of the classroom, and opened that door to reveal a narrow ascending stairway. Babylon climbed those stairs, followed by Einstein. At the top was a small office that had once been a janitor's closet. With his back to Julius, Babylon placed the key on the desk and opened a desk drawer to remove something from it. Then, he turned around, transformed by the addition of a Groucho Marx set of nose, glasses, and eyebrows. When he next spoke, his voice was shrill.

"Now, you have met Professor Hardaway. Sit down, and we'll start our interview.

The Groucho-masked face wore a sinister expression. "Frank Babylon never completed his PhD work at Harvard. He was expelled for plagiarizing his dissertation. He got angry about it, so he invented I. M. Hardaway to write some erudite papers ridiculing religions and God, including a few co-written by *Dr. Frank Babylon*." At this point, he smiled. "Terwillegar University academics were so impressed by those papers that they hired Babylon, hoping to increase Terwillegar's prestige as Babylon continued to publish in tandem with the illustrious Professor Hardaway. There you have it. Both of us must continue to exist. We're like a particle in quantum physics that can exist in two energy states at the same time. You do realize that we won't let you leave to publish our story."

Einstein smirked. "Both of those particle states are in front of me now." He wrote in his *causative* notebook: $e=mc^2$. Then he pocketed his glasses and suddenly appeared older and much taller.

As Hardaway/Babylon cringed, Einstein said, "You won't have to worry about my publishing your story, because I'm not actually a magazine reporter. I'm a much bigger problem for you. It's risky to make a career of ridiculing religions and God. By the way, *Lazarus has risen.* The police misidentified the body in that burning car. Martha's son Paul is quite alive." He took the key from the desktop and left.

As Einstein walked down the narrow staircase back to the classroom, the room above erupted with a muffled blast and a blinding flash of light in a tightly-contained bubble of energy. Einstein locked the lower door behind him, put the key in his pocket, and left the building to interview the next person on his list, a fertility specialist who fathered all the children born to his female clients.

NOWHERE AND NOTHING

Mary Pottyman swept the leftovers from the dinner plates into the garbage and carried the dishes to the sink for washing. They had eaten hot dogs and beans plus a salad, but somehow that simple meal had required a very large number of dishes. As she contemplated the dishwashing task ahead of her, Mary heard her husband Peter open the closet door, take out a jacket, and zip it.

"Peter, where are you going?"

"Nowhere; I just need some fresh air."

"When you get to nowhere, what are you going to be doing? Is nowhere the name of a tavern?"

"*Nowhere* isn't the name of anything. I'm just going out, and whenever I get somewhere, I'll be doing nothing in particular. I need my space." The front door closed behind him, and she heard him stomp down the apartment house stairs.

Mary turned her attention to the dishes. *Seven years they had been married, and almost every evening he had the same routine. Leave her to do the work while he went nowhere and did nothing. It was getting difficult to take anymore. It was bad enough that she had traded her maiden name, Wilson, for Pottyman. Her married name sounded like bathroom humor.*

After she finished the dishes and put everything away, Mary settled down to read the novel she had started last week, one by Stephen King. She enjoyed the way he created weird situations and worlds that were almost real but not quite. *Peter's going nowhere and doing nothing is almost like a Stephen King plot or a Twilight Zone episode. What could I do to shake him up a bit and make him relate to me and others better? What would Stephen King do?*

Mary slipped a bookmark into her novel, searched for a telephone number and made a call. She and the party on the other end exchanged comments and questions for ten minutes before concluding their conversation and a negotiation for payment. Then, Mary positioned her novel in a place of honor on her bookshelf, propped up to display the picture of Stephen King rather than the front cover.

When Peter eventually came home, Mary woke but didn't move from her sleeping position. *Maybe I'm overreacting. Peter isn't mean; he's just weird. I certainly don't think he has a girlfriend. Who would have him?* Peter's throaty "Grmff" as he flopped onto his side of the bed without getting under the covers, offset her charitable thoughts. Mary clenched her teeth as she drifted back to sleep.

The next evening, right on schedule, as Mary cleared the dinner table and began to wash the dishes, Peter declared that he was going out. They exchanged their 'nowhere' and 'nothing' litany, and he went out the door, slamming it behind him.

As Peter exited the front door of the building, he stopped and took a deep breath. Before he could exhale, two figures dressed in black grabbed his arms. A third individual slapped tape across his mouth stifling his protest and zip-tied Peter's hands behind him. The handlers guided Peter to a parked yellow van, pushed him into the back compartment, and locked the doors behind him.

The van's darkness surprised Peter. Then he realized there was a partition behind the driver and passenger seats preventing light from reaching him. He rolled from one side to the other as his eyes dark-adapted, trying to determine what else was in the van with him. The cargo space appeared to contain a few tools that clanged together as they drove and a rolled-up carpet. He couldn't tell whether the carpet's bulges indicated a bad rolling job or something inside it.

Peter tried to determine where the van was going by the few external sounds he heard, the smoothness of the roads, and the number of turns they took; but the long ride had so many deviations that he gave up and simply tried to remain calm. After what seemed like an hour but might have been less, the van turned off the paved road and headed down a rough unpaved winding trail. Ten minutes later, it climbed a small hill and stopped.

The rear doors of the van opened, and a back-clad figure pulled Peter out. A second figure retrieved some metallic sounding tools. They marched Peter up the hill to its top. Then they cut the zip tie on his hands.

Peter massaged his wrists and exercised them and his hands to restore blood circulation. He couldn't see any lights. He smelled a strange stench combining many different odors. One of his handlers placed a battery-powered lantern on the ground and lit it. Peter saw that he was standing on top of a hill of garbage. There was a thin layer of loose soil over most areas, but bits and pieces of trash protruded through it.

For the first time, a black-clad handler spoke – male, gruff, trying to lower his normal voice – "Start digging. We need a hole eight feet long, two feet wide, and three feet deep." He handed Peter a long-handled shovel and a pitchfork.

Peter nodded, tape still covering his mouth, and used the pitchfork to loosen the earth and garbage outlining the cavity he was to dig. As he worked, Peter saw the other two handlers carrying the bulging rolled-up rug from the van. *Hopefully, they plan to bury that bundle and not me. I wonder who's inside that carpet.*

Peter dug aggressively, feeling his muscles flex more smoothly with each shovel-full of debris. *If nothing else, this is good exercise.* The hill of garbage hadn't been packed down, so the work went more rapidly than expected. The three black-clad figures weren't watching closely, so he dug the hole wider and deeper than requested.

When Peter stopped digging, one of the handlers gestured for him to lift one end of the carpet-covered bundle. That handler took the other end, and they carried it toward the hole. Peter could feel the extra weight and stiffness inside the bundle. Together, they dropped the carpet roll into the hole. As he bent to drop his load, Peter grabbed the handle of the long-handled shovel he had placed nearby for easy access, and swung it to impact the carpet-carrying handler on the back of his head. That individual fell into the hole on top of the carpet.

The other two black-clad figures moved toward Peter as he pulled the tape off his mouth and grasped the pitchfork. "Now, we'll see how tough you are."

Peter plunged the pitchfork into the stomach of the first handler, and pulled it out quickly, dripping with blood and various other body fluids. The other figure turned and ran toward the van. Peter threw the pitchfork like a javelin and caught that person in the back. Both pitchforked figures twisted on the ground, yelling and moaning, at first intensely, but eventually decreasing to silence.

Peter dragged the bodies to the oversize hole he had dug. He unrolled the carpet to find a store window mannequin in it. He unmasked the black-clad handlers, discovering two men and a woman. Then he dropped them into the hole and shoveled the mixture of dirt plus garbage over them. When he finished, the ground looked undisturbed. Peter took out his cell phone, set the GPS app for home, and drove away in the van. He parked a few blocks from his apartment house and walked the rest of the way.

When he entered his apartment, he found his wife at the table doing a crossword puzzle. "You're up late, Mary. I thought you'd be in bed as usual."

"I wanted to learn how your evening went. Where did you go?"

"Nowhere."

She looked bothered. "What did you do there?

"Nothing."

Mary looked surprised but asked no further questions. Apparently, she was stuck with the 'nowhere' and 'nothing' routine. How boring!

A STUDY IN MAUVE

Hard-of-hearing private crime consultant, Sheerluck Holmes heard a muffled comment from his son John as he knocked his still-glowing pipe ashes into the fireplace. "What son? Come here. I need you.

When John arrived, he spoke quickly, before his father could pontificate about some abstract uselessness. "Dad, I've been meaning to suggest you change the name of your latest case. *A Study in Mauve* won't cut it with the younger crowd. If you change it to *A Study in Dusty Rose*, you'll at least appeal to females. Why did you call me?"

"Call Detective Inspector Lestrade, and ask him to come right over. I have a theory about a crime that will be committed tomorrow."

"How can you have anything to tell him about a crime that hasn't been committed?"

"Just call him as I asked. Tell him that he must come, or he won't be able to solve the crime when it occurs."

John left with a strange expression on his face, but returned five minutes later with a tranquil countenance. "Inspector Lestrade said he has better things to do than to listen to the proclamations of a raving lunatic. Those are his words, Dad. I'd never call you that. I do wonder, though, how you feel you can contribute to the solution of a crime that has not yet been committed."

"It's elementary, John."

"Right … but give me a hint."

"This afternoon, Mrs. Hudson received a visitor from the Bank of England, while we were both away."

"Did he, she, or they come because of a threat to the bank?"

"I wouldn't know. I wasn't here."

"Then why is your statement about the visit a valid hint about tomorrow's crime?"

"I said it was a hint, not a valid hint. It could be speculation. Speaking of speculation, did I tell you about next week's case about the *Speckled Band*?"

"Dad, you're starting to babble about many things at the same time."

"Good word, *babble*. Makes me think about the Tower of Babel in the Bible and about all the things people say to each other without an iota of shared understanding."

"Can we get back to what you wanted to tell Lestrade about tomorrow's crime?"

"It's elementary."

"You said that before."

"Do you want another hint?"

"Your last hint was useless."

"But wouldn't it be better to have more than one hint, useless or not?"

"I suppose. I'll humor you. Please give me another hint."

"A left-handed man with a right leg limp may be wearing a toupee."

"When he commits tomorrow's crime?"

"I wouldn't know, but I saw him getting a shoeshine yesterday."

"How did you know he had a right-legged limp if he was sitting down?

"Again, elementary. Extra wear on the toe and sole of his right shoe indicated he dragged it while walking. Are you sure you don't like *A Study in Mauve*?"

"I abhor it, Dad."

"*Abhor* is a pretty strong word. You win. It will be *A Study in Dusty Rose*. Thanks for your input, son. Now I have to make up my 3% solution."

"The only solution I want is the answer to how you know about a crime that hasn't been committed."

"It's elementary."

"Not that again. I want logic."

"Very well, John; you know my old adage that if you eliminate all the possible solutions to a problem except for one, that one has to be correct."

"But, Dad, I can't think of even one solution."

"I can."

"What is it?"

"I'm going to commit the crime, and Lestrade will never think I did it because I offered him the solution, and he refused to consider it."

Ten Minute Creation

I shot an arrow in the air;
It fell to Earth I know not where.
Critique Group wants me soon to read;
A subject I must find with speed.
Perhaps a poem about King Tut;
I'd rather write about a mutt.
Curled on my lap, he keeps me warm;
He knows he's safe from every storm.
Never laugh at a mongrel pup.
His love will keep your spirits up.
Your heart his love will fill with song.
Though impish, he can do no wrong.
Yet, when to doggie heaven he goes,
You'll see no end to grief and woes.
How to close that grief door shut?
Go out and get another mutt.

GOING TO
THE DOGS

"John, this has to be the craziest thing you've done yet!" Donna Callahan never minced words when it came to her obviously inferior husband.

"What's the problem this time?"

"You went to the groomer's to pick up Riley."

"Yeah. So?"

"The sheltie you brought home is female. It ain't Riley. How can you make a mistake like that?"

"If a mistake was made, the groomer did it. She handed me the dog. Then I put it on my leash and came home. All shelties look alike."

"Not to me. I'd know our Riley anywhere. Get this little bitch out of here and find our boy. I'd be better off with Riley for a husband instead of you."

John probed the dog's hair with his fingers. "She has a tag with her name, Ginger, and an address. I'll track it down and swap dogs. I'll be back soon."

"That other owner had better take good care of Riley. If he's hurt, I'll sue. We could use some settlement money."

"Don't worry about a thing." John left, harnessing Ginger to his car's seatbelt before he drove away.

The address on Ginger's tag, 3547 Maple Parkway,

turned out to be in a part of town that was beyond John's normal range. The white ranch-style house had blue shutters alongside the windows and a small front porch. He climbed the two steps to the porch carrying Ginger.

The doorbell was answered by a middle-aged woman whose hair was beginning its journey from sandy brown to gray. "Hello, I see you have a dog that looks very much like my dog. Are you wanting to sell it?"

"No, Ma'am. I'm John Callahan, and I'm here because this is your dog, Ginger. The groomer made a mistake and switched our pets. You have our Riley."

"Oh my goodness. I'm Mary Wallace. Just call me Mary. Please come in, John, and thank you for bringing Ginger."

"I don't want to upset your schedule. We could just switch dogs."

"Nonsense; the least I can do is make you a cup of coffee, or tea if you prefer."

"Coffee is fine. I take mine black without sugar."

"Have a seat, and I'll be back shortly."

John sat in an upholstered chair and smiled as both shelties jumped onto his lap. He could see Mary working in the kitchen, so he called out to her, "Our two shelties like each other. I have both Ginger and Riley on my lap."

"Have them get down and see whether they play together. I thought I had Ginger trained to stay off the furniture, but you must have been too great a temptation for her."

John gently pushed the dogs off his lap. They looked up at him quizzically, and then started to sniff each other. Following that ritual, they scampered around the room and then left for a different room.

"Mary, do you mind if the dogs run around in the

house. I could put them out in the yard if it's fenced."

"That's a good idea. It is fenced. Just be sure the gate is latched."

When John returned from the backyard, Mary had coffee and pastry on the table for them. As he was about to sit, his cell phone rang. He saw that it was from Donna, so he answered. "Hello."

"You must have gotten lost, picking up our dog. I have a bigger problem. The kitchen drain is clogged, and I have water spreading over the floor. What plumber should I call?"

"There's a new plumber named Venito in the strip mall at the corner of Main Street. He's the closest, and you might get fast service because he just opened up."

"You're never here when I need you, not that you know anything about plumbing. I'll call Venito. At least he's Italian, not Irish like you."

John apologized for the interruption and joined Mary for coffee. "Sorry about that. My wife had a plumbing problem, but she'll call a pro to fix it. At least I won't get blamed for it because I'm away from home."

"Blame isn't logical. You may get blamed for suggesting a plumber she doesn't like."

"You seem to know the ins and outs of marital squabbles."

"I'm a widow, John. Back when Walter was alive, I had more than my share of lectures about why I should do everything his way. He was a union boss, and he wanted to be a hard negotiator at home too. I named our dog Ginger because she always took my side and stood up to him. As soon as Walter started one of his tirades, Ginger would bark continuously, so that I could claim I never understood a word of it."

"It is hard to be on the receiving end of criticism all the time. I try to look beyond it. Let's change the subject and go see what the dogs are doing. Thanks for the coffee and pastry. They were both great."

When they went outside, the two dogs ran up to them, a quick check revealing that they had sorted out their ownership question, with Riley going to John and Ginger running to Mary.

"If you come back again, John, I'll put a red ribbon on Ginger to make it easy to tell them apart."

"I would like to come back again, Mary. You make good coffee. I'll be sure to bring Riley back too."

When John arrived home, Donna had a fan on to get the last streaks of water off the kitchen floor.

"Did Venito do a good job of clearing the drain?"

"Excellento! Much better than you would have done if you tried to fix it."

"I wouldn't have tried. I'm not a plumber."

"You're not much of anything. You take whatever job is available when you get out of work. Your problem is that you don't have any ambition."

"Well, hello to you too."

The next morning, John told Donna that he was going to get ambitious and walk at least one mile in the park every day. He would take Riley with him for company.

"Where is this park?"

"It's a new one I discovered recently, on Maple Parkway."

"That's fine with me. I don't trust you to help me around here anyway. You must have put something in the drain that clogged it."

"You should get a hobby or get away from the house

too."

"Yeah. I'll think about it."

About two months later, John came home with Riley after one of their outings. There was an envelope on the kitchen table with his name on it. He opened it to find a note from Donna.

Dear John:

Yes, this is a Dear John letter. I've had it with you. Since you decided to take long walks for physical improvement, you're not even around enough to give me the satisfaction of yelling at you. There's no purpose to our marriage, so I'm dropping you for Vinny Venito. You can keep the dog and what passes for our house. I'm partnering with Vinny in more ways than one. I'll be running his office and booking his appointments too. Money and I have been strangers in the past, but now I'll have plenty of it thanks to the wonderful world of plumbing. My lawyer will send you divorce papers to sign. Don't cross me up by refusing to sign. Vinny has some tough friends. Arrividerci.

John and Riley made it to Mary's house within the hour. "Donna's leaving me. We've become such close friends through our daily interludes. Will you marry me?"

"I guess I'll have to, for the sake of the children?"

"What children?"

"Ginger's pregnant. We're going to be grandparents to a litter of shelties."

"Wow! Both marriage and grandpuppies. Wonderful.

"Who is Donna hooking up with?"

"Vinny Venito, a plumber."

Mary laughed. "I told you my deceased Walter was a union boss. It was the Plumbers Union. He kicked Vinny Venito out of the union for embezzling their funds and branded him a crook. Vinny can't get a job with union requirements or a bank loan. His little company will never grow. Donna picked a loser."

"Well, I finally found a winner. Our dogs are a pair of Cupids."

PUBLISHER'S DELIGHT

Charles Penbury checked the address he had received in response to his email. It seemed to be correct, and matched the number on the building to which his GPS unit had guided his car. It was supposed to be PTL Publishing Corporation, but the building was unmarked and appeared to be a factory. *Oh well, they're probably a small firm renting unused space.*

His meandering journey seeking publication of his debut novel, *Love on a Carnival Ride*, had been strange but probably typical of those taken by many rookie authors. Seventeen query emails rejected by both large and small publishers – at least the smaller ones had responded with individualized rejections instead of form letters – followed by attempts to make in-person contacts with small presses suggested by author and barstool friends. Altogether, he had contacted thirty-one publishing gatekeepers before this visit to PTL Publishing. Hopefully, thirty-two would be his lucky number.

Charles parked and entered the front door of the building. He found himself in a tiny lobby with one chair for waiting visitors. There was a small sliding glass window with a dome bell on its counter board. Charles struck the plunger on top of the bell three times. He thought that would be adequate to attract attention, and that any additional rings would imply that he considered himself overly important.

A burly bearded man wearing a white T-shirt and blue jeans walked through the empty front office and slid the glass counter window open. "Hi. What can we do for you?"

"I'm looking for PTL Publishing. Am I in the right place?"

"Sure. This is a shared space venture incubator building. They're part of our family. Have a seat. I'll have them send someone down for you."

Charles sat as the man left the front office. *He said 'down', PTL must be upstairs. I wonder whether they're a recent startup too and if they have a track record.* He chuckled to himself as he realized that he was judging a publisher who would soon be judging him and his novel. *I sure hope they turn out to be a winner. They're the only publishers who thought I was worth a second look.*

He sat straighter as he watched the doorknob begin to rotate. *Show time!*

The door opened, and a red-haired woman in her early twenties walked in. She was wearing a blue sweatshirt and jeans, but in his mind Charles saw her in a bikini.

She reached out for a handshake. "Mr. Penbury? Welcome to PTL Publishing. I'm Phyllis Lansdowne. I'll take you to our conference room."

"Thank you. I notice that your initials match the company name. Are you the leader of the group?"

"We're a group of equals; there is no single leader. Your guess is creative, but my initials are not the meaning of PTL Publishing. Watch your step. We'll be going up a narrow enclosed wooden staircase. This building was once a bicycle factory, and many features of that history still exist, including the stairs to what was once the accounting office."

Charles entered the tunnel-like staircase and mentally thanked his hosts for having installed handrails on both sides of the steep stairs. He had to pull on the railings to hoist himself upward, while Phyllis navigated the steps unaided. At the top, they emerged into a brightly lit conference room with a large oval maple table. Four closed doors on the inside walls of the room probably led to offices.

Charles' eyes scanned the table. "How did you manage to get that massive table up here? There's no way it would fit through that enclosed staircase."

Phyllis smiled. "We hoisted it through a window. Take a seat, and I'll tell the others you're here."

Charles sat and placed his laptop computer on the table. *This is looking promising. I thought I'd pitch my novel to only one person. They're interested enough to have a group listen to me.*

Phyllis returned with two men, one of whom looked like a construction worker, while the other wore hand-tooled cowboy boots plus dress jeans and a leather vest over a bright orange shirt. She introduced them rapidly as they sat, and Charles mentally kicked himself for not remembering which one was Bill and which one was Ted.

Phyllis placed a tray of opened soft drink bottles in the center of the table and then invited Charles to begin his presentation. "I assume your computer has the manuscript in case we want to see the entire file."

He nodded his affirmation and stood because he had read that you're more in command when you look down at your audience and because he wanted to be free to pace off his nervousness. "Thanks for giving me the opportunity to make a personal presentation. My novel chronicles the life of a combat veteran who, after discharge, has trouble finding a well-paying job, so he becomes a con man who entices a wealthy woman to marry him. Once married, he takes her on an amusement park ride, has sex with her during the ride, and makes sure she *accidentally* falls to her death, leaving him all her money. Over the course of ten years, he repeats this process with three different wealthy women."

Ted/Bill with the boots asked, "How could he possibly get away with murder four times when he's repeating the same procedure?"

Charles expected that question. "He does it in four different countries that don't share their criminal files beyond their borders."

Bill/Ted the construction worker asked, "How did he know his wife wouldn't be able to push him out of the ride during sex?"

Charles finished his drink and put down the bottle. "He was very self-confident and had never lost a fair fight."

Phyllis shook her head. Her long red hair flew outward in a provocative manner. "I don't believe your plot is feasible. I don't think it's possible to have sex on an amusement park ride."

Charles smiled. "It is. I've done it."

Phyllis turned to Ted and Bill. "Are we ready in the next room?"

Bill/Ted the construction worker said, "We're ready when you are."

Phyllis stood, and the others followed suit. As they

walked through the door, Charles asked Ted/Bill with the boots, "What royalty structure do you have for authors?"

Ted/Bill with the boots said, "We haven't paid any royalties to our authors yet."

The next room turned out to have one wall missing, overlooking a three story open space in which stood a vertically circular carnival ride with horizontally swinging two-person seats that moved gently at slow speed of the circular wheel but could completely invert at higher speeds.

Ted/Bill and Bill/Ted escorted Charles to one of the seats and strapped him in.

Charles asked, "What is this, some kind of joke?"

Phyllis climbed into the seat next to him and fastened her seat belt. Bill/Ted the construction worker threw a switch to start a large growling motor.

Phyllis said, "We're going to find out whether you can have sex with me on a carnival ride and which one of us throws the other to the ground. By the way, our name PTL stands for Publishers Test Laboratories. I'm a combat veteran, and your drink in the other room was gently spiked."

THE DAY NOTHING HAPPENED

7:15 a.m. Usual start today. Clean up; store the bedclothes; plain Lithuanian rye toast and black coffee for breakfast. Weather check: looks OK somewhat cloudy.

8:10 a.m. Arrive at post office; check box mail; bills, junk, Express letter from UK.

Letter contents: Haiththwaite arriving from London 10:00 a.m. No email use - confidential.

Can't fit into schedule. Doris retired. Must man office. Text Martin to meet plane.

8:30 a.m. Arrive at office. Boot up computer. Review emails. Check Google News. Usual items.

9:10 a.m. Second cup coffee. Revise yesterday's annual report draft.

10:25 a.m. Text from Martin. UK flight arrived Chicago O'Hare. Haiththwaite not on it. Taken off plane at Logan Airport, Boston, complaining of neck pain. Texted back, Martin to coordinate with Boston hospital.

11:00 a.m. Email received. ER doctor told Martin puncture wound in Haiththwaite's neck. Appears to be poison injection. Haiththwaite now in coma.

Noon Ordered Chinese lunch special delivered and flowers for Haiththwaite's room. Alerted FBI of poison puncture diagnosis.

1:25 p.m. FBI email noting past connections between Haiththwaite and Russian poisoned politician Alexey Navalny. They are tracking Russian passengers on Haiththwaite's flight.

1:45 p.m. Called cleaning service. Told them office needs better cleaning tonight. Last week's cleaning worst in months.

2:20 p.m. Text from Martin. Haiththwaite's baggage and attaché case missing. Airport police checking surveillance videos.

3:30 p.m. Doris called. Not feeling well. Won't be at restaurant for her retirement party tonight. Perhaps another time.

3:45 p.m. FBI called. Three Russian passengers on Haiththwaite's plane. Two killed in gunfight behind their Boston hotel. One in custody. Leather glove with poison injector in their luggage.

4:37 p.m. FBI called. Russian courier arrested at Logan Airport, Boston. Tried to board flight for Moscow carrying Haiththwaite's attaché case.

4:45 p.m. Cleaning service email. Apologized for shoddy work. Promised to put fresh flowers in office for one month to compensate.

5:00 p.m. Leaving office after boring day just sitting at my desk. Will return Doris' gifts to Macy's on way home. Her retirement party now cancelled. Too bad. Was looking forward to it for something exciting on this day when nothing happened.

WATCH YOUR STEP

The doorbell rang long and loud. Mom started to get up from her comfortable recliner chair, but I reached over and put my hand on her arm. "Let Ralph get it. You don't want to miss any parts of your Hallmark movie."

Ralph was Mom's stubby second husband, acquired less than one year after my father died, probably too short a waiting period. He had a shuffling walk which, when combined with his short stockiness, reminded me of a pig on skis. I didn't like Ralph, but I couldn't stand in the way of Mom's wishes. I had to go along with her, but I didn't have to give their union my blessing.

I watched Ralph approach the front door, calling out, "I'm coming" as he walked. He turned the doorknob and swung the paneled slab fully open. I saw a look of surprise capture his face. Over Ralph's slumped shoulders I saw two large men staring at him, one in a police uniform and one in a suit.

The suit said, "We're from the police department. I'm Detective Malroney, and this is Officer Bratkowski. We'd like to talk with Ralph Grotz." He held up his identification card.

Ralph tried to look calm. "I'm Ralph Grotz. What can I do for you?"

"May we come in?"

"Certainly." Ralph moved to the side of the doorway.

I watched the detective scan the room as though trying to determine whether my mom and I might pose a threat. Satisfied that we were harmless, he turned back to Ralph. "We'd like to discuss an incident that occurred yesterday evening. Would you like to go to a private room to talk?"

I saw the color drain from Ralph's face. He looked nervous as he said, "I have nothing to hide. We can talk here. What do you mean by an incident?"

"We'll ask the questions. Were you at Crosby Park yesterday evening?"

I saw Ralph glance at me and then turn back toward the police. "I drove there looking for my stepson, Jerry. He hadn't come home for dinner."

The detective looked at me. "Is that true, son, that you didn't come home for dinner?"

I kept my facial expression blank. "I did miss dinner because I had late basketball practice at school. Mom knew about it, didn't you, Mom?"

My question came at a crisis moment in the Hallmark movie. "Sure. I remember you talking with me in the morning." Mom's eyes never left the television screen.

Detective Malroney turned back to Ralph. "What did you do at that park?"

"Nothing. I asked a couple of kids if they'd seen Jerry, and they said they hadn't."

"Were these kids boys or girls?"

"I don't remember. It was getting dark, and I didn't look that closely."

I saw beads of sweat on Ralph's forehead.

Malroney said, "Officer Bratkowski, tell Mr. Grotz what you reported."

"At 7:37 p.m. yesterday, at Crosby Park, two girls, ages

13 and 14 ran up to me and said that a short man in an old maroon van tried to lure them into his vehicle to see his puppy."

Malroney asked Ralph, "What vehicle do you drive?"

Ralph's shirt showed wetness from his sweat. "A Chrysler minivan."

"What color and what model year?"

Ralph's shoulders slumped more than usual. "It's a 2004 Maroon Town & Country, but I didn't see any girls or say that to them."

Malroney smiled. "You said earlier that you didn't remember whether the children you spoke with were boys or girls. Now you say you didn't speak to any girls. Which statement is correct?"

Ralph hesitated; then looked at his shoes as he muttered, "They were girls, but I only asked them whether they'd seen Jerry."

"Why did you say earlier that you couldn't remember whether they were boys or girls?"

"Cops are suspicious of adult men talking with young girls. I was being cautious."

I smiled as I watched Ralph's nervousness increase. His shirt was soaked with sweat. I wondered if he'd pee in his pants next.

Officer Bratkowski's radio beeped, and he went outside to take the message. When he returned, he whispered something lengthy to Detective Malroney.

Malroney faced me. "Jerry, tell me how you feel about your stepfather, Ralph."

I knew I'd be in trouble with Ralph if I was honest and in trouble with the police if I lied. The police scared me more than Ralph. "I hate Ralph, but I put up with him because Mom likes him."

"Did you set up the encounter in the park to get Ralph in trouble?"

I hesitated. "What do you mean?"

"The older girl, Patsy Morgan, had second thoughts about the story she told Officer Bratkowski. She said you asked her, in exchange for money and a future date, to say Ralph tried to lure her into his van. Is that what happened?"

Now, I was the one who was sweating. "It's true, but I had to do something to get Ralph out of here."

Malroney looked serious, bordering on angry. "Jerry, I don't know whether you realize it, but making a false accusation and fabricating evidence are crimes. I'm going to have to take you to the Police Station for further investigation."

The Hallmark movie having ended, Jerry's mom tuned in to the last few discussion points. She stood and addressed Malroney. "Detective, I don't think you see the whole picture. Jerry went about this in the wrong way, but he's only a youngster calling out for help."

Malroney couldn't help noticing how tall and attractive she was when not slumped in an easy chair watching television. "What am I not seeing, Ma'am?" He couldn't believe he'd used that term of address – too much time spent watching Dragnet shows when he was a kid.

"Ralph Grotz is an alias. My second husband's last name is actually Granitz. I learned that recently while doing family genealogical research. Ralph Granitz went to prison for being a pedophile. He should be a registered sex offender, but he thinks he can hide from the law within our family. Regardless of what Ralph did or didn't say to those girls in Crosby Park, he was breaking the law by being there with them. Jerry was feeling uneasy around his stepfather, and he had every right to be nervous, given the pedophile conviction. Ours is a fraudulent marriage, and it's time for me to end it."

Detective Malroney asked Ralph, "Is this true? Did you serve time for being a pedophile?"

Ralph said nothing, but looked down at the floor.

Malroney gestured to Officer Bratkowski. "Read him his rights and take him down to the station. I'll finish up a few details here."

I stared at the detective. "Am I in the clear? I'm sorry I staged that business in the park, but I needed to get that weird guy out of here without hurting my mom's feelings."

"You're cool, Jerry. Go tell your friends they're not in trouble either."

After Jerry left, Malroney turned to his mother. "If you see Officer Bratkowski again, don't mention it to him, but I enjoy Hallmark movies too. By the way, I'm Larry, and I never did get your name."

"It's Trish, and the best part about Hallmark movies is that they all have happy endings, Larry."

THE SECRET OF ETERNAL LIFE

Carl Patterson Looked up from his notes and stared directly into the Zoom camera. "As applied to human beings and other living creatures, the second law of thermodynamics says our bodies must eventually break down, and every one of us must die, sooner or later. There is no way to defeat the physics of the situation, but I have found a way to sidestep it."

He looked at the mosaic of pictured Zoom attendees on his computer's screen. He had certainly grabbed their attention with his declaration that he could promise eternal life – that is, he had grabbed all but one of them. Everyone on the mosaic of screens looked intent and appeared to be leaning slightly forward except for a young red-headed woman. She looked bored as she leaned back and took a drink from her bottle of Dos Equis beer.

Carl continued his presentation. "Our history and literature are full of attempts to prolong the human life span. Vampires accomplished it by drinking the blood of younger people. Ponce de Leon claimed to have found the Fountain of Youth. In more modern times, doctors have tried hormone replacement therapy and have somewhat extended lives through organ transplants. None of these approaches have resulted in the extension of lives beyond the accepted limit of 125 years. The longest actually recorded lifetime was an individual who lived 122 years from 1875 to 1997."

He glanced at his computer screen. The red-headed woman had left her work station. *After that beer, she probably needed a bathroom break. I hope she doesn't have a worse problem with her drinking than that. It's only 9:30 a.m.*

"Concerning that list of past attempts to prolong life, I'd have to say that the successful accomplishment of organ transplants and their societal acceptance have been major accomplishments. As with automobiles, we can simply replace worn-out parts to rejuvenate our bodies. Unfortunately, as we age, we find that there are too many discrete parts of our bodies needing replacement, and we have no answer to the failure of our internal control systems rather than individual organs."

Patterson nodded to the camera person, and the camera panned from his face to a cart bearing a large object covered with a heavy black cloth.

"Today, I am pleased to announce that my associates and I have solved the problem of extending human lives without limit. Furthermore, we have demonstrated the technology through its application to several test individuals."

The images of the Zoom audience on Carl's screen showed even greater attention, and he noticed that the red-headed woman had returned from her break.

The camera returned to focusing on Carl. He removed a handkerchief from his pocket and wiped off his glasses. "Before I go into the details of our research, I need to address some philosophical aspects of life. Extending the lifespan of a person without maintaining good quality of life is not beneficial. It is cruel to force a person suffering from poor health to continue facing pain and mental anguish forever. For this reason, our new technology will only be offered to seniors who have relatively good physical and mental health. It will not be available for everyone.

"A second philosophical matter is the nature of human life itself. For purposes of the application of our research, we have postulated that what makes humans uniquely thrive is their ability to think and store information. Our scientific name is *Homo Sapiens*. *Sapiens* is the Latin word meaning wise. None of the other primate groups have the brain power or, to the best of our knowledge, what we have termed the mind or soul of man."

The camera followed Patterson as he walked over to the cart with the shrouded object on it. "Our approach to increasing lifespan is humane and follows in the footsteps of those who transplant organs." He removed the black cloth and let it fall to the floor, revealing a red opaque spherical object that resembled an oversized crystal ball or snow globe. "Ladies, gentlemen, and those of nonspecific genders, please appreciate that you are the first outside of our research group to see our intermediate mind transfer system, which we call *The Sponge*."

The mosaic of attendee images on Carl Patterson's computer screen showed everyone leaning slightly forward, even that red-headed woman.

Carl's voice bloomed with enthusiasm. "Our technique is basically similar to the heart transplant procedure in which the donor organ is kept beating by a machine until it can be successfully implanted within the recipient's body. We have a more complicated system because we do a two-way transplant of minds with both donor and recipient alive. Please note that no one dies during our procedure. We capture all thoughts, memories, and beliefs of an older person, and store them in The Sponge. Then we do the same for the mind contents of a younger person. Then we switch the polarity of The Sponge to implant the older mind in the younger person and the younger mind in the older person. Without deterioration, the senior individual continues his or her life within a complete younger body, while the younger individual moves on to the retirement phase of life with a fresh youthful outlook. The procedure is repeatable when the newly occupied younger body eventually wears out. Hence, we can achieve eternal life."

Carl noticed a question symbol on his computer screen. He unmuted that person's microphone.

"Dr. Patterson, I'm Lyle O'Brien, and I find this concept of transplanting a mind hard to accept. Why should we believe you?"

Carl unmated another individual and nodded to the camera operator.

The red-headed young woman began to speak. "Mr. O'Brien, I can assure you that the system works, but it's not perfect. I was a seventy-five year old man, and now I'm a twenty-two year old woman. They wanted to see what would happen with a gender change, and it's messed up my thinking. Getting used to being female is difficult. I have to learn about new body functions, and my sexual urges are cross-wired. I also enjoyed spending most of my spare time fishing, and my new body has allergies that won't let me touch live bait."

O'Brien responded, "How do I know you're not a paid actor and that this isn't a snake oil medicine show? It will take more than one testimonial to convince me."

Carl Patterson smiled. "I expected that this young woman's case study would be sufficient, but perhaps I was a bit naïve. I didn't plan to reveal more of our progress today, but perhaps I should. You've seen one example of an older mind in a younger body. We've actually done a large number of mind transplants. We've found that for young minds transferred into older bodies, it works significantly better for men than for women. Join me next week for tours of a retirement center and a local church. At that time you will see numerous examples of senior men who think they are still young and able to do many things beyond the capabilities of their older bodies."

THE LETTER

As he scanned the morning mail in his post office box, the author paused when he saw the profile of Queen Elizabeth II on the stamp. He rarely received mail from the United Kingdom, and this letter bore his address written in an extremely neat style, probably by a feminine hand. He left the post office and sat in his car to read the unexpected missive.

Dear Sir,

I've just finished reading your novel, Impostor, and I felt compelled to contact you because our respective stars appear to have crossed paths. I realize that your novel is historical fiction and that its details originated in your imagination, but I have been struck by the fact that your female protagonist lives in a house that is very much like mine and is located in my village of Upper Benefield. Is this coincidence, or were you a resident of my area in a prior life? I would greatly appreciate receiving your views on this strange situation. As a further stimulus to your thinking, consider the fact that my grandparents moved here from Massachusetts about fifty years ago. I know you have Massachusetts roots. Perhaps you knew my grandparents or have some past connection to them.

Please do not consider this a trifling letter from one of your fans. I am quite normal but seriously intrigued by the fact that I appear to reside within your novel.

I will look forward to your response.
Yours faithfully,
Evelyn Washburn
P.S. By way of preliminary personal information, I am a
31-year-old nurse.

The author replaced the letter in its envelope and held it up against his forehead, as though trying to divine some mystical connection with it. *If only the name Evelyn Washburn didn't sound so familiar.*

He drove to his home office and searched his notes for the novel, *Impostor*, for any mention of Washburn or Evelyn Washburn. He didn't find anything. Next, he pulled several genealogy files to see if they contained someone named Washburn. He didn't find that surname, but he discovered that his maternal grandfather had divorced a woman named Evelyn before he was born. The possibility of a genealogical connection with the letter writer would be slim, but he was between projects and able to waste a little time on this puzzle.

At the end of her letter, Evelyn Washburn had included her email address. The author went to the *compose* section of his email program, entered her address and then "PUZZLE" on the subject line. He limited his message to one question. "Were you named after one of your ancestors?"

Ninety minutes later, he received a reply. "I had to ask my mother, but it turns out I was named after my father's grandmother, who would have been my great-grandmother. Her name was also Evelyn Washburn."

He emailed a prompt reply. "She may have been my grandfather's divorced first wife, remarried. Was her maiden name Crowder? Even if so, I don't understand how it would cause an unknown distant relative to be living under the circumstances contained in my novel."

The reply relieved his building tension. "No, her maiden name was Murphy."

His next emailed question took a different approach. "How long have you lived in your present location?"

The response surprised him. "It's quite late here. I'll reply in the morning."

The author wrestled with the coincidence puzzle in his dreams. When he awoke at 6:00 a.m. he went directly to his computer to receive Evelyn's message. For her, it would be about noontime. The email contained the answer to his previous question. "I've lived here almost four years, but I only recently read your novel."

He started to smile as he replied. "I have a key question. How did you obtain your copy of *Impostor*?"

When he read her response his smile broadened. He wrote back, "Mystery solved. You indicated you purchased the house furnished and recently found my novel in the bookcase. It appears that the estate agent who sold you the house was an early fan of my novel, and he or she planted a copy among the other books for you to find at a later date. Do you have a continuing friendship with that estate agent?"

The next email from Evelyn Washburn read, "I'm so dim. My estate agent was my cousin Rodney. He set me up for a fall. I'll bet he didn't put that novel onto the shelf until he last visited with the rest of the family at Christmas. This has been one extremely long prank."

The author responded once more. "I've enjoyed our exchanges. One-up Rodney by telling him we're now close friends, and that I'm looking forward to visiting you when I do my British book tour next year. It's time for me to make an appearance in Upper Benefield anyway.

At the next family gathering, Evelyn cornered her cousin away from the others. "Rodney Templeton, you planted a copy of that *Impostor* novel in my bookcase. You knew I'd realize my cottage and location resembled those of Alice in that story. Why did you do such a sneaky thing?"

"Good, you found it. I wasn't sure whether I was being too subtle. I did leave it protruding a bit to draw your attention."

"What do you mean by subtle?"

"Your home wasn't the only parallel to the *Impostor* story."

"Explain yourself."

"Well, Evelyn, in that story, an undercover Churchill agent, using the name of Michael Farrell Hadley, pretends to be Alice's brother and moves in with her while he is in training for his next assignment."

"So?"

"Shortly before I added that novel to your bookshelf, I learned that I was adopted and that I'm neither a Templeton by birth nor a blood relative to you. I'm a pretender also."

"Did that discovery disappoint you?"

"Hardly. I've cared about you in an uncousinly way for a very long time, but I've had to properly subdue my feelings. Now, like the fictional Michael warming to Alice, I'm free to tell you that you mean ever so much to me. I hope you'll come to feel the same way about me."

"Rodney Templeton, you are sneaky and have a weird sense of humor, but I'm sure I'll eventually come to cherish those traits."

From the open doorway, someone observed, "We

have a pair of kissing cousins in the family."

WHAT CREEPS
IN THE NIGHT

Whatever wriggles in the night
Over your toes or out of sight
Can cause completely irrational fright
It's dark and so unknown.

I clench my fists with all my might
Determined to hold back that fright
I close my eyelids very tight
And whistle in a cheery tone.

And then I hear a movement slight
Coming from somewhere to my right
It's my new puppy, Silent Knight,
He's chewing on a bone.

I grab that pup and hold him tight.
This time he wriggles out of fright.
And then he knows he'll be alright
When I give him a scone.

THE CHRISTMAS MOUSE

Twice under the space (I'm tired of "once upon a time.) bar of an old contraption called an Underwood No. 5 manual typewriter, a mouse named Algernon sat eating his favorite potato chip crumbs. Not only was *The East Parsonsfield Monthly Express* (TEPME) the least frequently published periodical in Maine, but it was also the shortest. The writer/editor/publisher of TEPME, Frank Incense had once written novels about the glorious adventures of world traveler Aaron Gold, but now he spent his senior years producing TEPME and inadvertently feeding his accidental pet mouse Algernon.

Algernon worried about Frank, partly because his writer friend was getting more than a little absent-minded, but also because Frank thought imaginary things were real. Algernon frequently heard Frank discussing the future with a space-traveler friend from somebody else's novel, Meredith Myrrh. It was obvious from Frank's babbling that he was in love with Myrrh, even though the time dimension kept them forever separated, because she will be from the future.

Algernon didn't quite understand why Frank and Meredith, being from two time periods, couldn't get together. After all, Frank through his writing regularly communicated with Aaron Gold who was from the past, again a different time period.

Algernon decided to arrange for Frank and his friends to get together. Algernon was a very smart mouse indeed, for he had eaten a whole roll of SpaceX rocket drawings, and he had digested all the information on them. He built a rocket out of old Pringles Potato Chip tubes filled with a mixture of flour saturated with all the printing press cleaning solvents he could find. He topped off the rocket with a stack of Aaron Gold novels and placed the whole assembly under Frank's bar stool out back by the barbecue.

The next evening, Christmas Eve to be exact, Frank went out back to roast his Christmas goose, and sat on his bar stool while it was cooking. Algernon ran a fuse from the barbecue fire to the rocket under Frank's stool. That is how the goose facilitated the combination of Frank Incense and Aaron Gold shooting up into the cosmos at a speed great enough to distort the space-time continuum so that they united with Meredith Myrrh. Past, present, and future blended in an intense burst of light that looked like the brightest star ever.

By its light Gold and Frank Incense and Myrrh, now thrown well into the past, looked down at the earth and witnessed the birth of a Special Baby. What surprised them most was that they saw Algernon kneeling down before the infant along with several farm animals. Their favorite mouse must have stowed away on the rocket but bailed out early.

JACK AND JILL

Jack and Jill went up the hill
To fetch a pail of water.
Jack fell down and broke his crown,
And Jill came tumbling after.

Don't look now, but this story sounds phony to me.

Water flows downhill. Ponds and wells are generally found at the bottoms of hills, not at the tops of them.

So, what were Jack and Jill doing at the top of that hill? I suggest that they were playing grown-up games.

Why else would Jack have fallen on the way down? He didn't have his trousers all the way back on, and they tripped him.

Jill tried to catch him before he fell, but she had a wardrobe malfunction too, and hence came tumbling after.

Now, there's a key phrase. "After what?" I ask you. It must have been after they had sex at the top of the hill.

And why at the top of the hill? Because their parents would have a hard time climbing up to catch them and because Jack and Jill would see people coming before they reached the top.

Since there probably wasn't any water at the top of the hill, they probably carried beer in their bucket. Kids grow up too fast nowadays.

FATHER GOOSE RHYME (SECOND VERSION)

Jack and Jill went up the hill,

To fetch a pail of water;

Jack fell down, and broke his crown,

And **Jill** came tumbling after.

That's strange ... water flows downhill. Why would you go uphill to get some?

The updated version is:

Jack and Jill went to a pub

For libations and some grub.

Jack staggered out and lost his keys.

Jill tripped over Jack down on his knees.

HISTORY

History, His story, God's log of the world.
The women yell, "Her story" ERA banners unfurled.
We try to think back to where we've all been.
Future folk look at us and what we have seen.
Past, present, and future - they're one and the same,
For living's our goal. Scorekeeping's a game.

THE COCKTAIL PARTY

Hank had to remind himself why he was here. It was expected of him. For some strange reason, his deceased girlfriend, Marianne, had included in her will a provision that Hank would have to attend this reunion cocktail party to learn the exact nature of her bequest to him. The fact that there even would be a bequest struck him as weird. As far as he knew, Marianne was a struggling grad student, holding down two part-time jobs to afford the rent on her one bedroom apartment in a century-old building. Maybe the prize awaiting him was non-monetary, like a pet dog or cat. The dog would be fine, but he wasn't much of a cat person.

He had dressed casually – jeans and a sport shirt plus sneakers – assuming that the people in the small town of Baileyville, Maine, population 1318, would be informal. He wondered whether any of the guests would be from Canada, since one of the town's borders was the international dividing line.

Setting all speculations aside, Hank approached the specified address and parked in the driveway of a newly-constructed two story house. He was surprised to find the available driveway space because the street was lined with the parked cars of other guests. Perhaps someone in that spot had left on an errand. He accepted his good fortune and approached the front door. As he reached for the doorbell, he saw the sign: *Go directly to backyard*. Hank followed the sign's arrow around the right side of the building.

As he turned the rear corner of the house, Hank passed under a banner that read, *Marianne's Party*. This struck him as unusual but touching. Marianne had died two months ago, but her friends in Baileyville were still celebrating her life. He was even more surprised when the guests in the backyard applauded as he appeared. Not knowing what else to do, Hank said, "Thank you, I'm Hank Turner."

A middle-aged blond woman stepped forward. "We all know who you are. I'm Sylvia Willingham, Marianne's mother. Marianne sent me monthly slide shows of her outings with you, and I shared them with all my friends. I hope you don't mind. You may feel like a stranger here, but to us, you're almost part of the family."

"Marianne didn't tell me about that picture sharing. I was always amazed at the number of photos she took, but I never questioned what she did with them. I probably should have asked her. Anyway, I'm here as requested. I'll celebrate her life with you."

"She was special in many ways. This is too large a crowd for introductions, so you'll find that everyone here has a large print nametag. You won't have to squint to see their names. Help yourself to a drink from the ice chests and some snacks at the long table. Then mingle with our Baileyville folks. We'll have a bit of a program later."

The drink selection was varied, with pre-mixed cocktails, wine coolers, and many local craft beers and ales represented. Hank selected a twenty-two ounce bottle of Gritty's Ale to minimize his number of return trips for additional drinks. He doubted that anyone would count those trips, but he wanted to make a good impression. As he left the table with a handful of mixed nuts, Hank saw a man with a badge on his belt approaching him. Hank stuffed the nuts into his mouth and wiped his right hand on his jeans so that he would be able to shake hands. He managed that ritual, but had to hold up his index finger in a *pause* gesture while he finished chewing the nuts.

The man with the badge chuckled. "Take your time, son. I wouldn't want your first visit to Baileyville to be marred by a choking episode. I'm Tyson Jenks, the police chief, and before you ask; yes, my mother named me after a package of chicken."

Hank nodded as he finished chewing. "That was a case of bad timing – my mouthful of nuts, not your name. Glad to meet you, Chief. From the little I've seen of it, Baileyville is a peaceful old town."

"It is old, but we have a way to go to earn the peaceful label. Even though we're small, the latest statistics show that we have a higher crime rate than 84 percent of U.S. cities. We once had mostly property crimes, but in recent years we've seen all-too-many in the violent category. Sometimes, I think television makes small-town folks imitate big-city people. Anyway, we're hiring another couple of officers to try to get things under control."

Hank realized his casual comment had struck a nerve. "I'm sure you'll get there, Chief. Are parties of this size common around here?"

"Not so much among older folks, but we frequently have to break up wild parties among the youth. They use social media to attract out-of-towners."

Hank realized he had again triggered an unwanted discussion. He excused himself to get another snack, but headed for a woman sitting under a tree instead. He was rusty at party talk, and he hoped his next conversation would go better. As he approached, the woman started to stand.

"Please keep your seat. I just wanted to join you in the shade."

"It is a bit warm. I'm Martha Pence. I was Marianne's American History teacher in high school."

"That's interesting, Mrs. Pence. My high school didn't even teach American History."

"It's Miss Pence; just call me Martha. Your high school was probably not in one of the New England states. History is a big deal in New England."

"You're correct. I'm a Midwesterner, and they mixed History with other subject matter under the Social Studies title."

"Don't worry. The longer you stay in New England, the more American History will rub off on you."

"That sounds like an easy way to learn about the past, but I'm only here for the party and perhaps an extra day or two. Given my short visit, I'd better mingle with a few more people. I'm glad I had the chance to meet you, Martha. By the way, was Marianne good at History?"

"She was the best student I ever had."

Hank mentally kicked himself for never having become fluent in the language of party conversations. He approached a young couple based on the theory that chatter would come more easily with three people involved. Before he could reach them, someone rang an antique schoolbell and shouted that everyone should gather by the food table for the planned program.

Marianne's mother, Sylvia Willingham, stood next to a video monitor which was cycling the photo images that Marianne had shared with the Baileyville home folks. As the pictures continued to change, she welcomed all the guests, pronounced Hank Turner to be the guest of honor, and invited him to stand next to her. Once he arrived there, she said, "This party is a celebration of Marianne's life and a ceremony to welcome her friend, Hank, into our midst. Please raise your glasses and join me in that welcome."

Everyone cheered, and those who had glasses or bottles raised them in a welcoming salute.

Hank waved his appreciation. "I've never had such a greeting, and I'll remember it forever. Marianne was very dear to me, and we were beginning to plan our joint future when she had that terrible car accident that led to months in the hospital and ultimately took her from us."

Sylvia asked, "And where were you planning to spend that joint future?"

"We didn't get that far into our dreamwishing, as Marianne called it."

"Do you think Marianne wanted to live here, in Baileyville?"

"With all due respect, I always considered her a city girl. I didn't even know she came from this small town."

"Hank, I don't know whether you noticed when you first arrived, but there is a sign on the front of this house that is covered with a cloth. There is an identical cloth-covered sign here, on the rear of the house. Would you do me the favor of removing the cloth from this sign?"

He didn't know the purpose of this exercise, but Hank walked over and pulled the cord attached to the cloth sign cover. Once the cloth fell, he realized that something special was happening. The sign read, *Dreamwishing Manor*. He stood in silence and then said, "I thought that only Marianne used that word."

"She did, but she wanted to share it with her special someone – you. While she was in the hospital, Marianne asked us to build this house for you, Hank. It's yours now."

He stood shell-shocked, but everyone else applauded and cheered.

"I can't accept such an expensive gift, and sign or not, I can't go dreamwishing without Marianne."

From behind him, a female voice said, "Stay; and I'll help you remember her."

Hank turned around and felt weak. "Marianne, how can you be alive?"

Sylvia smiled. "She never told you, but I had twin daughters. This is Julianne, Marianne's twin."

Julianne approached Hank and gave him a light kiss on his cheek.

"Unbelievable; you even wear the same perfume."

"We enjoyed shopping together as we grew up."

"I don't know what to say. The house is still too much to accept."

Julianne smiled a duplicate Marianne smile. "My sister said you wanted to buy a house for her. Isn't it a bit sexist to be shocked that she bought one for you instead?"

"There is a difference between a house that two people share and one that contains only one person plus memories of the other."

Sylvia said, "That's why we're here today and will be available whenever you want us in the future. We're going to give you flesh and blood memories of Marianne. Through us, you'll be seeing her on a daily basis. You'll know what your life with her would have been like."

"I have to go back to my job. I have to support myself. You're all very generous, but what would you get out of my living here in this house?"

Sylvia laughed. "Several career opportunities have been lined up for you in this area. Our benefit would be lively memories of Marianne, and we'd get to share our lives with the man she wanted to marry. You do realize that when you marry someone, you're committing your life to her family and friends also."

"Before Marianne died, that thought did cross my mind, and I wondered whether her family would accept me, coming from a different part of the country and an unusual background. I guess I have my answer. It's good to feel wanted."

"Then you'll stay to live in Dreamwishing Manor?"

"I'm not sure, Sylvia. I can see possible problems ahead."

"What kind?"

"If I immerse myself in your family and town, and keep replaying memories of Marianne, I can see myself confusing those memories with the living person of Julianne. That wouldn't be fair to her or to anyone else."

Julianne squeezed Hank's hand. "Let me worry about that problem. Marianne and I shared all our secrets."

Hank stiffened and stared at her. "That hand squeeze was exactly like Marianne's. Are you sure you're her twin sister and not her ghost?"

CHOCONOMICS

I propose a new worldwide currency based on chocolate as the unit of value. Unlike a cryptocurrency such as Bitcoin, my chococurrency would be based on something real and valuable, in the same way that diamonds undergird the jewelry industry.

Some might say that the two are entirely different, because there is essentially a fixed supply of diamonds, making them rare, while more chocolate can be manufactured on a continuing basis.

My response is to base my new currency on vacuochocolate, a very special variation that can only be formulated and created in the vacuum of outer space, requiring a very expensive and specialized orbiting factory. Its most novel characteristic is a matrix of vacuum bubbles within its dark brown strata. This matrix could not be duplicated in an earthly laboratory or factory. The purpose of the vacububble matrix is to continuously enhance the value of this form of currency. Eating vacuochocolate causes you to lose weight because vacububbles remain in the human body indefinitely, causing surrounding atmospheric pressure to compress your flesh as it pushes your exterior inward to fill your internal vacuum..

The owner of chococurrency would continuously be tempted to consume his or her currency in order to lose weight while also reducing the total supply of the new means of exchange, making it more valuable in the marketplace. However, one's personal supply of chococurrency would be small compared to the total worldwide supply, so temptation might quickly lead to one becoming a poor person with a svelte figure. Thus, the overwhelming problem would become, "How do I have my chococurrency and eat it too?"

GAMES

The thump woke Harry from his mid-news-broadcast nap. It sounded like a huge icicle breaking loose from the rain gutter. Then the fog of sleep lifted enough for him to realize it was April. He looked out the door and saw that he had a package. The delivery person must have thrown it against the door. He would have considered filing a complaint if he had actually been expecting something.

Harry took the carton to the kitchen table and cut the tape with a paring knife. When he looked inside, he saw large plastic air bubble packing material but not much else. After Harry set all the packaging bubbles aside, he saw a clear plastic box on the bottom of the carton. His pulse rate increased when he realized it was a puzzle box with money inside. It was the type where one had to manipulate a steel ball into a certain position on the lower level of a maze in order to release the latch on the drawer that held the money, in this case a one hundred dollar bill.

Harry looked at the internal plastic maze, shrugged his shoulders, and opened his tool drawer. He placed the puzzle box on the floor and smashed it with one blow of a hammer. Then he pocketed the bill, swept the clear plastic fragments into a dust pan, and emptied the swept-up contents into the kitchen trash bin. He treated himself to a can of beer and sat in front of the television to watch the baseball game.

Three innings later, he was awakened from a nap by the ringing of his doorbell.

Peering through the side window, he saw his neighbor, Ethel Gilbert staring at his front door.

Harry brushed his hands over his hair and eyebrows before opening that portal. "Hello, Ethel, it's been quite a while since we chatted. What brings you over to my house?"

"I came home expecting to find an important UPS package, but it wasn't there. Our neighbor, Dwight, said he saw UPS make a delivery to your house. Is there any chance that you received my shipment by mistake? It's a birthday present from my sister."

Harry remembered that he hadn't examined the address label on his surprise package. He asked Ethel to wait in his front room while he checked. When he picked up the carton by the back door and read Ethel's address, he knew he was in trouble. He remembered instructions from his Army days to always have his lies contain a certain amount of truth. Reluctantly, he fished the hundred dollar bill from his pocket, put it in the carton, and retrieved most of the broken pieces of plastic from the trash bin to add to the box contents.

He carried the open container to the front room where his guest waited. "Ethel, I made a mistake. This package arrived today, and the contents sounded broken, so I opened it without reading the address. It must have had rough handling during shipping. The box is dented too from being thrown at my front door."

Ethel examined the contents, saw the hundred dollar bill, and smiled at Harry. "I'm so glad to have an honest man as my neighbor. I'm the one who should apologize. You've been living here for two years, and I've never brought you a housewarming gift or invited you to my place for coffee. I promise I'll be a better neighbor in the future. Several of us are going out for pizza on Saturday. Please join us."

Harry thanked Ethel as she left. Then he took a fresh beer and returned to the televised baseball game. *I stole a base safely that time. I never thought of Ethel as a potential friend. She likes pizza. If she turns out to like beer and baseball, we might have possibilities.*

STORM

(Written at age 24)

Swirling, whirling, twirling,

Blur upon the sea -

Whistling undulations buffet buildings –

Strewing broken boards upon the beach.

Shoreline trees, their finery in shreds

Weave in frenzied dance

To the pounding rhythms of the sea.

Ever greater grows the pace as aged giants

And spindly saplings cower

Under the grotesque whips of broken power lines.

Yet all is not chaos and destruction,

For within a small but sturdy structure,

Safely sheltered from the buffeting billows,

A soft, significant sound is heard.

Quietly and without concern for chaotic tensions

Life reasserts itself, as a tiny girl-child

Takes her first breaths and proclaims this world good.

CAGED

(Written at age 24)

What's that shrieking and thumping?

> The little bird is trying to escape.

Why is she locked in a cage?

> They say she's very sick.

Who are they?

> The people who know about such things.

What do they say is wrong with her?

> They say she is infected.

With what?

> They don't know – something new and different.

Will she get well?

> She thinks she's well now, but they don't agree.

Who is right?

> They both are – It has something to do with what they call qualitative and quantitative. In terms of qualitative, she's well as she says. In order for her to be quantitatively well, she has to play a game with them and hit a *magic number*. Then they'll let her out.

It's all very scientific.

Why does the bird object?

She claims that she's part of the old system wherein qualitative wellness was enough.

What a funny outlook!

I heard them say that she's a throwback to earlier times.

Oh … Poor little bird …

MATURITY

(Written at age 24)

Maturity, a word of awesome depths
And facets of many dazzling hues.
How to cope with gradual awakening
To such a weighty force,
The mere incantation of which
Evokes Responsibilities ...

The shudder past,
The youth recoils to familiar warmths
Like firesides, overstuffed chairs,
Or the magnificent splendor of the sun-tinged hills.
Can he face independence in a society which
Claiming stringent standards, cherishes none?
Can he face the prospect of having to use human beings
And find himself inhumanely used by others?
And can whatever code he forges and bonds to his image
Sever ponderous barriers like enchanted blades of old?

A staggering load of questions appears to be

The only prop on which to rest new maturity.

But perhaps the youth will find, as others have before

The magic of the humorous touch; through humor lies Excelsior!

SPATTER

Licking my peppermint ice cream cone brought back the image of Jeff's dog licking his master's spattered blood from the white carpet when I first arrived at the scene. They had ruled Jeff's death a suicide but I couldn't buy that conclusion. Jeff always hated guns and wouldn't have tolerated leaving this world with one in or near his hand. He was also a neat freak.

When Jeff first stated that he was going to buy a white carpet, I told him he was crazy because he'd never be able to keep it clean. He responded that he had purchased a variety of carpet cleaning tools and solvents and that he was looking forward to tackling the whiteness challenge. He even bought slip-on booties for his miniature schnauzer, Junior, and planned to use them every time they completed an outside walk.

Jeff's neatness actually bugged me over the years, but I learned to endure it, even though it made me uncomfortable. He would have cringed at the idea of leaving this life in his immaculate personal space with a gun in his hand and blood on his carpet. If Jeff had decided to commit suicide, he would have drowned himself in Lake Michigan or driven his car into a concrete bridge support.

I know the medical examiner's conclusion is wrong, but how can I prove it to her and to the police? They're all too happy to consider the case closed because of all the street violence investigations they have on their platter. I also have no special investigative skills. I'm just a librarian.

The one benefit of the suicide ruling and the case closure is that Jeff's house is not considered a restricted crime scene area. Suicide isn't a crime. Further, Jeff nominated me several years ago to be executor of his estate, and he gave me a house key in case he was hospitalized, so that I would be able to care for Junior.

The police completed their brief examination of Jeff's house and then removed his body. I arrived shortly before they left and volunteered to make the required identification of his body because he was a widower with no relatives in the area. Following the identification, I took Junior back to my place for easier care and made arrangements with a funeral home to handle Jeff's cremation after the police released the body.

When Junior and I returned to Jeff's house several days later, we found the bloodstained carpet had been removed. Even without that living room floor covering, Junior spent five minutes sniffing and licking the bare wood where the police had discovered Jeff's damaged body. Following this initial examination, Junior raced upstairs to his master's bedroom. When I reached that room, the schnauzer was under the bed, pushing something around and barking. I knelt down and moved Junior aside so that I could retrieve the object of his anxiety.

That item turned out to be Jeff's cell phone. I surmised that the police hadn't bothered doing a thorough search of the house once they reached the suicide conclusion. Apparently, the pistol found near

Jeff's hand trumped the usual expectation of a suicide note.

I knew where Jeff kept his secret notebook full of passwords, so I located it and found his PIN number for activating the phone. I wasn't surprised to discover it wouldn't work without a battery recharge. I'd feed and walk Junior on his home turf and then do an overnight phone charge when we returned to my place.

I examined Jeff's phone while drinking my morning coffee the next day. My first check was to call it from my phone to see if the recorded message indicated anything about Jeff's state of mind. After five rings I heard his recording. *At the tone, you may leave a message plus your name and contact information. If I know you, or if your message is convincing enough, I may return your call. No promises. I'm usually quite busy, so I set priorities for tasks to be done.*

That message in Jeff's voice caused Junior to bark continuously and run around the room several times. It convinced me that Jeff was planning a continuing future when he recorded it, but it probably wouldn't convince the police that he wasn't suicidal.

I next called his voice mail number to hear his incoming and stored messages. Most of them were either innocuous or spam, but one caught my attention. *I'm calling because I found your number many times in my wife's call history, sometimes when you called her and others when she called you. We've had our troubles, but I'm trying to get back in her good graces. Stay away from her and stop calling. Don't get me angry. I have friends you won't want calling on you.*

Finally, I had something that might make the cops reconsider their suicide conclusion. I called Detective

Quinn who had given me his card when I went to identify Jeff's body. When he answered, I said, "I have new evidence."

"Evidence of what?"

"Sorry, I got excited and skipped the preliminaries. You folks ruled Jeff Perkle's death a suicide. I knew him for many years, and suicide didn't fit his nature, so I've been checking further."

"What are you, an FBI profiler?"

"Nope, just a research librarian, but I found Jeff's cell phone, and it has a threatening message on it."

"Play the message for me."

After I played the message, Quinn chuckled. "That could be considered a threat, but I think the caller's a desperate husband trying to checkmate the competition. He doesn't sound violent to me, and he probably doesn't really have criminal friends. The case is closed, and I'll need more than that message to get it reopened. My advice is that you accept the suicide verdict, but I'll listen if you come up with more convincing evidence. That's the best I can do for you."

I reviewed the rest of the voice mail messages on Jeff's phone and located those from the wife of the threatener. Her name was Audrey, and she sounded interested in Jeff romantically, but she also seemed to want to use his skills as a chef for several planned parties.

I called Audrey, informed her of Jeff's death, and inquired about her husband's message. Her response was accompanied by anger and more than a few tears.

"That so-called husband of mine, Gregory, is a jealous ass. We're officially and legally divorced, so he has no business objecting to my friendship with Jeff. There's no way in hell that I would want Greg back in my life."

"Do you think he would be capable of murdering Jeff or hiring someone else to do the dirty work for him?"

"Jeff was murdered? You didn't say that earlier. As to Gregory, he's a slimy snake that crawled out from under a rock, but I don't consider him dangerous."

"The police think it was suicide, but I can't believe that, and I'm trying to learn more about his situation. Did you and Jeff have any major arguments?"

"Don't look at me as a possible culprit. We didn't even disagree on party menus. His situation, as you put it, was that we were planning our first vacation together. We were going to leave next Sunday for two weeks in Las Vegas. Jeff wouldn't have committed suicide to avoid going with me if he changed his mind. He could have simply phoned. I'm with you on thinking he must have been murdered, but not by me. How can we prove it?"

I caught the implication that I now had a partner in my investigation. "Do you know anyone who hated Jeff or had a grudge against him?"

"He had an argument with a Dodgers fan when we went to a Cubs game, but they didn't even know each other's names, and no one murders because of a baseball squabble. He also said he lent money to an old acquaintance for a business venture, and that person refused to pay him back, even though his new restaurant was doing well. That old friend wasn't you, was it?"

"Nope. I eat at restaurants. I don't run them. That unpaid debt might be a motive for murder. Do you remember the name of the restaurant?"

"It was Antonio's, but the owner's name was different. I think it was Fergus or something like that."

"Jeff knew a guy named Stan Berges, and didn't trust him. He's a chiseler who always bends the rules to his own advantage. I met him only once a couple of years ago. He fits the profile of someone who would borrow money and then try to get out of repaying it. Let's check him out. Can you meet me for dinner at Antonio's?"

"Best offer I've had all day. How will I recognize you?"

"I'll wear my 2016 Cubs World Champions shirt. By this time, they're rarely seen in public. I'll look for you to wear something red."

"Don't forget that you haven't introduced yourself except as Jeff's old friend. What's your name?"

"George Paul; sorry I didn't mention it before."

"I'll assume that's your real name, but if you mention friends named John and Ringo, I'll raise an eyebrow."

"I'm for real. I'll meet you at Antonio's at six o'clock."

At six sharp, I was leaning against a light pole in front of Antonio's wearing my Cubs championship shirt, when a dark-haired woman wearing a Boston Red Sox shirt approached me. "Audrey?"

"Yup. I figured I'd better join you in the baseball motif, so that we'd look like a matched pair. Let's put eyes on this welcher who might have shot Jeff."

We went inside Antonio's and sat at a booth in the back corner. I prefer to have solid walls behind me when dealing with a potential murderer. We ordered overpriced hamburgers. I recognized Stan and pointed him out to Audrey. He was arguing with a vendor nearby, next to the kitchen swinging doors. I set up my phone to make a video of their conversation.

"Look, there's no way you're going to get the rest of the money until you give me another case of beer. The labels on that last case were scratched and torn."

"They weren't torn when they were on the truck.

Your waiter must have damaged them during the unloading process. He's as big a chiseler as you are."

"Watch your accusations. That waiter is my son."

"No wonder he's as mean and devious as you. Keep that case of beer. You're cut off for credit. If you want any more beer from us in the future, you'll have to pay up front before anything leaves the truck."

"Watch your step. The last guy who pressured me for money ended up regretting it. You wouldn't want to have an accident."

"That does it, smart-ass. Your account is cancelled. Buy your beer from someone else." The vendor left through the kitchen and never looked back.

I pocketed my phone and focused my attention on Audrey so that Berges wouldn't think I had been listening. Audrey was quite attractive and had a good gift of gab. We were getting to know each other better when Stan Berges approached our booth.

"Is everything all right here? I haven't seen you two here before."

I responded before Audrey could. "It's our first time. I saw your sign, and it reminded me of my grandfather Antonio, so we decided to give you a try. Are you short on kitchen help? Our hamburgers are taking a long time."

Berges left, went into the kitchen and yelled at someone, and then came back out to flash us a thumbs-up signal. Then he disappeared toward the other end of the restaurant.

Audrey patted my hand. "Good job. I thought he was going to accuse us of eavesdropping. He sure is a nasty bastard."

"No guarantees, but my video may be enough to get the detective to take another look at Jeff's death as a possible murder. I'd like to go back to your place and make a video of you summarizing what Jeff told you about the loan to Berges and his refusal to pay it back. That will help our case with the detective."

The hamburgers weren't bad, but we concentrated on getting to know each other rather than the food. When we left the restaurant, Audrey gave me a slip of paper with her address in case I had trouble following her home. As she turned to walk back to her car, she said that she would expect to learn more about Grandpa Antonio after we returned to her condo. The evening visit to her place turned out to be more than pleasant, but I successfully avoided picking up on her occasional romantic cues in deference to Jeff.

The next morning, videos transferred from my phone to a USB flash drive, I called Detective Quinn to schedule a visit. He said he could give me a half hour just before lunch. I rushed to the police station before he could get too hungry to pay attention to my arguments for reopening Jeff's case. Over coffee, I summarized Jeff's relationship with Audrey and views on Stan Berges. Quinn nodded and wondered out loud why Jeff would have loaned Berges money in the first place. I guessed that Jeff, as an amateur chef, had a soft spot for anyone opening a restaurant.

Quinn watched the videos without comment. Then, he entered Stan's name into his computer and searched his police records. "We've had a bunch of complaints about Berges over the last six years, usually based on fraud allegations, but there are also a few assault incidents. This guy doesn't shy away from violence."

"What did you think about his telling the beer vendor

that the last person who pressured him for money ended up regretting it? It's not quite a confession, but that person was most likely Jeff."

"I don't always appreciate an amateur detective trying to do my job, but I know this Berges is a nasty piece of work, and that on-camera statement is close to damning, whether it refers to Jeff or someone else he beat up or killed. You win, George. I'll put in a request to reopen the case, at least with regard to investigating Berges as a murder suspect. I can't guarantee that we won't return to the suicide verdict, but this guy is certainly suspicious, and I'd like to nail him for something. He's slipped through the cracks and avoided prosecution on all his earlier complaints. Thanks for the videos. I'll keep you informed if we get results."

I called Audrey from my car when I stopped for lunch. "Thanks for all your help. The detective reviewed the videos and says he'll recommend reopening the case to investigate Stan Berges as a possible murder suspect. I feel much better now. I owed this investigation to Jeff."

"*We* owed it to Jeff. Don't plan on casting me aside now. It was fun working with you. We should do more together."

"If you're suggesting we should become private detectives, I'd have to spend a lot of time thinking about that."

Don't forget, George, we'll have to spend more time on Jeff's case if the police rule Berges out as the murderer."

"I already said I'd have to think about whether I want to do more investigating."

"You can start next week."

"What do you mean by that?"

"I still have the tickets and hotel reservations for that

vacation in Las Vegas I was going to take with Jeff. I wouldn't want to waste them."

"Sounds interesting, but I can't go. I have to dog-sit with Junior."

"Junior was part of our plans. We're booked into a hotel that welcomes pets."

"You do seem to think of everything, Audrey."

"I told you, we'll make a great team."

THE SHARK AND I

A shark swam up to me one morn,
He was large but quite polite.
He said he hadn't eaten all day,
Would I mind if he took a bite?
I said he'd have to come onshore
So I could sit on my 3-legged stool.
When he asked why, I said with a sigh,
It's part of my golden rule.
He wriggled ashore but said he'd have to eat more
Because of his extra work.
I sawed him in half and broiled him with a laugh
I'll eat him with coffee I perk.

MORAL: Even sharks should learn that what you do unto others
may someday be done to you.

DETOUR

"Bradley, I have an appointment downtown this morning. I just stopped in to pick up the file folder I need."

"Mr. Rush, today is the tenth. Remember, you're supposed to meet with the Employee of the Month to deliver a bonus envelope."

Ratchet Science had started small. In the beginning, it easily fit into the third floor of a loft building upstairs from the blind broom makers who were upstairs from the casket manufacturer. Over the years, Ratchet Science had ratcheted up in size until it now needed three buildings to house its operations and employees.

"I don't have time to go out into the factory to make a presentation. We'll have to delay the award until tomorrow."

"I think I have a way for you to do it today. This month's award-winner is Carol from Accounting. She eats breakfast every morning at Estelle's Restaurant. It's only one block out of your way. Just stick your head in there, give her the envelope, and get back on the road."

"All right, I'll do it that way. I have so few personal contacts with employees nowadays that I need to show I care."

Carol Stephenson didn't need the extra cup of coffee. Her edginess had been obvious to Linda, her favorite waitress. Work was hard enough without the additional caregiver tensions. Her mother had been extra demanding this morning after a sleepless night. Sometimes Carol thought her mother spurned her diabetes diet just to be spiteful. Carol wondered whether, as a child, her mother had played the spoiled brat when she had been the dependent one.

Work was another problem. Everyone at work knew that Ratchet Science had over-expanded. Sales had diminished to the point that the possibility of layoffs had threaded through all the cafeteria conversations for the past two weeks. Nobody official had said anything on the topic, but rank and file employees knew when to get nervous. Carol couldn't afford to lose her job, and she certainly wouldn't be able to tolerate spending twenty-four hours each day with Mother. She adjusted her posture and took five deep breaths, letting them out slowly, to see if it helped her outlook the way that magazine article said it would.

Don Rush entered Estelle's and scanned the patrons for a familiar face. Once he saw Carol, he gave the hostess cash to cover her meal cost and went over to join her.

"Good morning, Carol."

"Good morning, Mr. Rush; I don't remember you here for breakfast before."

Don sat down. "Actually, I'm not here to eat. I'm here to see you. Bradley told me this is your regular breakfast stop. I'm pleased to inform you that you've been selected as our Employee of the Month."

"That's wonderful, Sir, but I had no idea I was even under consideration."

"That's a deliberate Employee Relations tactic. They

figure that everyone will work harder if they all think the monthly award is a possibility. Anyway, I'm pleased to give you this envelope containing a one thousand dollar cash bonus. Thanks, Carol, for your loyalty and service to Ratchet Science."

Carol realized that her hands were shaking. She gripped the edge of the table, hoping that Mr. Rush wouldn't notice. She felt her face reddening.

"Thank you so much, Mr. Rush. I'll use it toward my mother's health problems. My day just got so much brighter."

Carol, I have to head downtown for a meeting, but I'm extra impressed that you do such a good job at work and take care of your mother too. Here's one of my special business cards. I call it my *Get out of jail free* card. It has my personal note on the back of it. You give this card to Sam Walker in Personnel, and he'll arrange for you to receive a promotion within your department.

"I do have to get on the road now; thank you again for all your good work,"

Carol sat there flabbergasted. Not only had he freed her from fear of a layoff, but he had also recommended her for a promotion. The money would be useful too. This had turned into one of the best days of her life. She had dreaded to have to lead today's defect-reduction meeting in Production Control, focusing on their latest ratchets for the Stanley tool line, but now she felt energized and sure that they'd pinpoint the problem.

At a booth on the other side of Estelle's Restaurant, Carol Murphy from the Accounting Department waved to Linda to bring a coffee refill. Carol knew she'd need it as extra fortification for the tedious day she faced, preparing for the auditor's visit.

Linda filled her cup and asked, "You work at Ratchet Science with Carol Stephenson, don't you?"

She works in Production Control, and I work in Accounting. Why?"

"Your chief honcho came in while she was eating, paid for her breakfast, and gave her some kind of award."

Carol Murphy leaned back and shrugged. "Some people have all the luck!"

As Don Rush left Estelle's, he caught a glimpse of a second familiar face at the other side of the restaurant. He had climbed into his car and driven seven blocks before the face registered – Carol Murphy ... A second Carol ... Had Bradley said Production Control or Accounting?

Don called Ratchet Science and told them to get both Bradley and Stephani from Empoyee Relations on the line for a conference call. It took three more blocks of Don's travel before they both got on the line.

Don used his gruff boss tone. "I decided this morning that I've been short on personal contacts with individual staff members. In the old days, I handled the selection of the Employee of the Month, instead of delegating that function. I've decided to resume that responsibility."

Bradley said, "Fine, Mr. Rush, that's a good idea. It will help morale among the troops."

Stephani said, "And when are you you taking that responsibility away from me, Don? When is your decision effective?"

"It's effective immediately. I've already implemented the change. This month's selection is Carol Stephenson and, in deference to your handling this function up to this point, the selection for next month will be Carol Murphy. I already feel better about enhancing relations with the staff."

Stephani said, "Bradley, you can hang up now. I have confidential Employee Relations matters to discuss." [… click…] "Don, you're the boss, but you owe me something for chopping one of my responsibilities. You'd better mark your schedule for some enhanced staff relations at my apartment this evening at seven o'clock … This invitation is effective immediately."

PART TWO – NONFICTION

LOSS OF INNOCENCE

Bobby and Billy were my close friends. They were brothers who might have been taken for twins, especially when they both wore their sailor suits. Bobby and I were in first grade together, while Billy was way up in the third grade. One unique aspect of this school relationship was that while Bobby and Billy weren't twins, their teachers were. Our first grade teacher and Billy's third grade teacher, both named Miss Rask, were unmarried redheaded identical twin sisters.

After school, whenever we had time and permission, we would play together, frequently at Bobby and Billy's house instead of our three-room apartment. Their house was an old gray New England colonial type with a basement that included a no-longer-used coal bin, converted into a studio for their father, the first artist I ever met. He knew he had found an enthusiastic audience in me, and enjoyed showing me the basics of oil painting as well as his pet white mice.

Social norms were different in 1944, both because the background for our lives was the Second World War, and because people respected authority and had no qualms about letting children run free. This was Boston, where even unaccompanied children traveled by bus and streetcar to local and special destinations and walked long distances to school and friends' homes and movie theaters.

One unusually warm and sunny autumn day, Bobby and Billy's father took them by bus to the Charles River near Harvard University, where he set up his easel to paint a view of the college, while the boys played on the grassy, tree-lined bank of the river. It was a perfect day for almost any activity, and occasional lounging college students completed the tableau.

The boys played and raced along the riverbank for about an hour, attracting little attention. Then they discovered a treasure. Billy found some short boards, left over from a construction project. These would make perfect boats. Each brother took a board, and found a tree branch. Then they went to the edge of the river, where they each put a board into the water and shepherded it along the shore with a long tree branch.

This Navy game continued without incident for about fifteen minutes. Then Bobby's board boat floated out beyond the reach of his tree branch. He decided to wade in after it. The shock came when the water depth increased sharply two yards from the shore. Then he discovered that the peaceful appearance of the water's surface belied the strength of the river's current. Bobby yelled for help.

Billy looked around for adults, but saw none. He hesitated for what felt like forever. He knew he had to help Bobby;

his dad had told him to take care of his younger brother. He didn't want to go into the river, but he knew he had to risk it. Billy shouted to Bobby that he was coming. He took his boat-herding branch into the water with him, hoping that Bobby would be able to grab it before the water got too deep. He waded, probed the bottom with his stick, and extended the stick toward Bobby. Then he waded, probed some more, and reached again. Then his feet could no longer touch the bottom.

The next day, Mom asked me to sit beside her on the couch. She showed me the newspaper, folded to show a particular article. *Brothers Drown in Charles River*. I couldn't believe I would never see them again. Bobby, Billy, and I had been inseparable friends, doing everything together. I cried for longer than I'd ever cried before as Mom held me in her arms. So this was the meaning of death – endless separation.

APRIL FOOLS' DAY 2020 – A COVID-19 LAMENT

April Fools' is cancelled this year,

As we self-isolate with coronavirus fear.

Wash those hands when you touch the mail.

Discard all envelopes without fail.

Hooray, we received a food delivery,

But making it safe will get me quivery.

Suds wash all apples and other fruit.

Discard all bags and cereal box to boot.

To serve take-out food in your own bowl is great.

Throw out their wrappers and microwave plate.

When out to the pharmacy, use their drive-through,

Where masked med techs look through the plate glass at you.

Order everything useful or wishful online,

But your credit card bill total will not be fine.

Ordering clean wipes, gloves, and TP's not okay.

They're all out of stock. Happy April Fools' Day!

ON WRITING
OR NOT

Am I a writer when I do not write?
If writing is my vocation or profession,
Why do I have to clear my desk and minor tasks
Before I enter words into a digital machine?
Why do I feel guilty when I steal priceless minutes
At my desk when others want me to do family things?
I lose that guilt when I abandon words
In favor of serving other folks,
But deep inside it hurts,
Even when telling party jokes.
Not writing is like skipping church,
Religion given less priority.
I must instead write unabated,
For "In the beginning God created..."

ON EBOOKS

Ebooks represent the future in that they are more than print books. You can branch and link out of them and then return to your reading content. In my novel *Impostor* I branched out to a ten minute movie that the Brits made to show how resilient they were despite the Blitz and to encourage the US to enter WWII to support their cousins across the pond. The film was part of the story and added another dimension to the book. In the future, more books will be written in a multimedia mode. It's not appropriate for every book, but expect to see more of this.

BOOK EVENTS: WHY, APPROACHES, AND GLITCHES

Why Events?

A few years ago, I interviewed Marshall J. Cook, writing coach extraordinaire at the University of Wisconsin (now very actively retired) and author of many books, fiction and nonfiction. Among many other gems he offered was: "POD [Print On Demand] and ebooks have opened up publishing incredibly and made book publishing much more economical and less wasteful. That said, it has made it tremendously difficult for any one title to receive any attention and find its readers. (The problem has shifted from getting published to getting noticed.) When I first started teaching, there were 65,000 books published that year in America (about a tenth of them fiction). The number is now ten times that! (with the same ratio of fiction to non-fiction). Average sale of a POD self-published book is 147 – but millions of people are selling them, so the so-called tail of the marketing dragon has become huge."

Add to the *getting noticed* argument the fact that very

few traditional publishers currently offer substantial marketing services to any but their celebrity and bestselling authors, and you have a good incentive for staging events and becoming personally known to readers and potential readers.

Approaches

The first principle of staging an event is that it, like your book, should be entertaining. It is only secondarily an opportunity to sell something. Most readers want to meet an author, learn how he or she thinks, and perhaps ask some questions. They also appreciate receiving something at your gathering, whether it is food/drink, a handout document, a souvenir, or a raffle ticket for a free book. Marketers will tell you that people who receive something are more likely to buy something.

The most traditional of book events takes place in a bookstore and may have the format of a reading, an informal discussion, or a lecture. The format usually depends on the facilities and the interest of the bookseller. It may take place during normal business hours or in the evening after the store has closed to the public. In either case, the critical keys to success are a diplomatic and low key approach to the bookseller, sufficient lead time to fit the store's schedule, and a clear understanding of who is responsible for furnishing the books to be sold.

Perhaps the most enjoyable event is one that is tied to the content of your book. My Lord's Prayer Mystery Series and my Imp Mysteries feature a continuing cast of characters and an ongoing joke about a Chinese restaurant called House of Ming that is owned by Tony Fleming, who learned to cook Chinese food in Chicago and truncated his name to gain an oriental atmosphere. This offered me the obvious option of staging events in Chinese restaurants, with delicious benefits for my attendees. The restaurant approach works well if they have a private room, but may be difficult in the main dining room unless you have an intimate group.

If you want to sell books, your best opportunity may be to stipulate that desire in connection with a speaking appearance. This may augment the honorarium you receive, and it offers exposure of your books to people who have already indicated their interest in what you have to say. You should, however, realize that sales may be limited to brief break intervals plus time remaining at the end of the meeting. Speeches to other writers may be your best opportunity, because writers tend to support each other and enjoy learning techniques from others.

A valuable variation on selling books at a writers' meeting where you are the speaker is the shared adjacent event. A few years ago, I joined with two other members of Off-Campus Writers' Workshop (OCWW) who also had new books out, to rent an adjacent room immediately following an OCWW session. The event took place at noon, so we provided tasty snacks and shared the hour with three short presentations and sold books at three separate tables.

It's important to be creative. If you can build your event around a setting or incident in your book, do so. You will also find that one event may trigger another. I did an evening presentation at a bookstore that was attended by several members of a Sherlockian group. They later approached me to address their gathering. I doubted that they would purchase many books (They did buy some.), but I used the event to generate and distribute charts comparing various authors' detectives including

Sherlock, other classic sleuths, and my own Pastor Arthur Blake.

Whatever events you organize, remember to always follow up with a summary on social media. The fact of each event, regardless of its economic value, enhances your authoring brand. Keep your followers talking about your books and your activities whenever practical.

Glitches

Book events don't always turn out well. Here are a few of my personal miscues.

- After my first book, I was offered a bookstore talk during the break of a speech by a better-known author, and I turned it down.
- I announced an evening event at church, and no one came.
- I had a Sunday afternoon slot at Centuries and Sleuths Bookstore on a March day that was the first 80 degree day of the year, following a bitterly cold winter. The gathering was small.
- I did an event at a bookstore where I supplied the books. They moved to a new location two weeks later and lost thirteen of my books during the process.
- I negotiated a future sales table at a bank in connection with my self-help book *Decision Time!* The banker took the free copy of my book, but never scheduled the event.

Events allow you to meet your readers and potential readers. They build your brand. No matter what happens, you learn from them.

I'M MY OWN GRANDPA

There's a novelty country and western song called "I'm My Own Grandpa." I invite you to listen to it now, as sung by Ray Stevens. Grandpa Song

I heard this song many years ago, and I thought it was very clever, but hardly realistic. Little did I suspect then, that in a sense, it would apply to me.

During the past several years, I've consulted various genealogy services to find out a few more facts about my ancestors. These services feed huge numbers of old documents into large computers so that you can search for your relatives by names, dates, places, special events, etc. One of the things they don't tell you is that when you enter information about your family, they share that data with other individuals and with other genealogy services. That's all fine when sharing permission is granted, but they share mistakes as well as true information.

I won't identify the specific service I used a year or two ago, but their instructions for starting a family tree were not clear. They had me enter my name and birth date, and then they told me to enter my earliest known relative. I entered the name of my father's mother. At that point I must have hit the RETURN key or done something else that was incorrect, because the system displayed a two-box family tree that showed me married to my grandmother. I looked for editing tools to correct the error, but I couldn't find any, so I simply abandoned the project. A few of my cousins had developed family trees, and I could always consult theirs.

About a month ago, I received an email from this genealogy service suggesting that I check my family tree because new information had been added to it. I clicked on their link and discovered that the service had added boxes to my old two-box mistaken start of a family tree. I was still shown as married to my grandmother at the top of the tree, despite the fact that the data indicated that I was born nine years after my grandmother died. My father and his siblings were shown as my children, my father having a different surname due to bad penmanship by a census-taker for the 1920 Census. This incorrect surname appears to have been shared among many different genealogy services, reinforcing the error and making it appear legitimate. Underneath my father's box on the tree are my sister and I.

THUS, it has been established by a leading genealogy service (and probably shared to the other companies) that I'm my own grandpa.

THE CEMETERIES
OF GETTYSBURG

On an elevated stretch of Taneytown Road (PA Rte. 134) in Gettysburg, Pennsylvania, sits Evergreen Cemetery (originally dubbed Ever Green). When it was organized in 1854 because of its bucolic setting and scenic view, the dedication speaker, Reverend John H. C. Dosh remarked, "Could a more lovely spot have been chosen?" Actually, the official designation for this cemetery's location was Adams County, Pennsylvania, both because it was a rural setting and because the name of the adjacent town, Gettysburg, did not convey any special significance or emotional overtones.

Now described in its brochure as *Gettysburg's most historic cemetery established 1854*, Evergreen thrived prior to its abrupt encounter with destiny during the first week of July of 1863. An ornate arched gatehouse was constructed in 1855. Prominent families who lost loved ones during this period constructed tall monuments and obelisks to mark the graves of their departed kin. The location of Evergreen became popularly known as Cemetery Hill. Prior to the establishment of Evergreen it had been called Raffensperger's Hill, taking its name from the farmer who had owned the land.

Evergreen Cemetery and Cemetery Hill had major roles in the Battle of Gettysburg. The first day's fighting on July 1, 1863 began at McPherson Ridge, west across the hamlet of Gettysburg, population approximately two thousand at that time. At about eight o'clock that morning, Union cavalry discovered a column of Confederate infantry moving eastward along Chambersburg Pike. The two forces fired upon each other, initiating three days of military hell. Additional forces from both sides came to aid their brothers-in-arms as soon as the terribly primitive communications systems allowed. On the first day of the battle, the Confederates had the upper hand because their forces greatly outnumbered those of the Union, and the bluecoats retreated, losing the day's battles, but gaining the long-term advantage by seizing the ring of high-ground positions along the eastern border of the battlefield: the hills called Big Round Top, Little Round Top, Cemetary Ridge, and Cemetery Hill. Cemetery Hill and Culp's Hill formed a convex fishhook anchoring the Union positions on the northern end of the line.

Once the Union forces had successfully retreated to command the arc of high ground surrounding the battlefield, the Confederates knew they were at a decided disadvantage. General Lee summoned General Richard Ewell and accused him of disobeying his orders to take the high ground of Culp's Hill and Cemetery Hill. General Ewell took his reprimand without comment. His forces had been weakened and scattered after earlier fighting against Union troops, so he had chosen to use them against Union units he had a chance of defeating, instead of attacking the stronger, entrenched units on Cemetery Hill. Ewell had been accustomed to the no-leeway orders of General Stonewall Jackson who had died two months earlier. In contrast, Lee's orders were usually politely framed as suggestions, and in at least one instance earlier, Ewell had earned a victory by assaulting a target Lee had told him to avoid, without receiving any subsequent criticism from his superiors.

Questions remain as to the degree of planning and coordination of General Lee with other Confederate forces. One could argue that the Confederates had the opportunity to deny Union control of Cemetery Hill because on June 26, 1863, five days before the first shots of the battle, Lt. Col. Elijah V. White's Confederate cavalry had taken control of Cemetery Hill and had captured horses that people from Gettysburg had hidden there to avoid the animals being confiscated from their farms. White and his men then departed for York, Pennsylvania. If Lee's strategy were really to make an all-out effort to strike the Union on its own soil in order to make them go on defense instead of offence, wouldn't he have coordinated his actions with those of other Confederate troops in the same area?

Speculations aside, the Union forces did gain control of Cemetery Hill and Evergreen Cemetery. The gatehouse was used as headquarters of the XI Corps by General Oliver O. Howard. He and his men tried to be good stewards of the cemetery, reclining most of the taller monuments onto the ground to minimize the damage they might receive from incoming artillery strikes. Cemetery Hill was a perfect artillery platform, commanding the fields and roads lying between it and the ridges that bounded the fields on the west (Warfield and Seminary Ridges). XI Corps artillery units positioned their cannon for the pending battle while their infantry units built defensive trenches against Confederate assaults. The artillery power at Evergreen Cemetery was later enhanced by six Parrott 10-pound rifled cannons of the Fifth New York Light Artillery. These rifles had a range of five thousand yards at twenty degrees elevation, and were able to strike the entire path of the advancing Confederates during Pickett's charge on the third and final day of the fighting, July 3, 1863.

During the three days of fighting, about one third of the combatants became casualties. 7,058 died (3,155 Union and 3,903 Confederate). 33,264 were wounded, an estimated thirty percent of whom probably died later from their wounds (14,529 Union and 18,735 Confederate). 10,790 were missing (5,365 Union and 5,425 Confederate). At least two of the Confederate casualties were women disguised as men. At the end of the fighting, the fields and surrounding hills were strewn with bodies of men, mules, and horses. State militiamen were assigned for several weeks to keep the battlefield secure from looters and curious civilians, collect military weapons, and to assist hospital as well as cemetery personnel. Initially, the dead were buried temporarily where they had fallen. Those who could be identified were typically marked with a board carrying a penciled inscription. About 5,000 horses and mules had died during the battle. They were burned in huge funeral pyres, creating a long-lasting stench over the battlefields.

Land on the southern border of Evergreen Cemetery was set aside for a new military cemetery. Initially and officially named Soldiers' National Cemetery, it is today more popularly called Gettysburg National Cemetery. The Union dead who were not taken home by their families are buried there, along with a few Confederates. Almost all of the Confederate dead remained in temporary battlefield graves until southern veterans' societies relocated 3,200 of them to cemeteries in southern states during the 1870's. The Union graves are arranged in a concentric semi-circular array by states, surrounding the central Soldiers' National Monument. The sections for soldiers from New York and Pennsylvania are the largest because those states contributed the most soldiers to the fighting. A large monument at the north end of the cemetery commemorates the dead of New York. Pennsylvania waited until this monument had been constructed before building a much larger memorial to their soldiers on Cemetery Ridge. Beyond the semi-circular array of Civil War graves, the balance of the cemetery land contains graves for military veterans of more recent wars, a few of the older gravesites including space for wives.

At the far southern end of the National Cemetery is a monument commemorating Lincoln's Gettysburg Address during the dedication ceremony on November 19, 1863. The sign on that monument indicates that the speech was given 300 yards away. What it doesn't say is that the platform from which Lincoln spoke was actually in the adjacent Evergreen Cemetery. A current brochure from Evergreen says that lots are available for purchase *near the site of the "Gettysburg Address"*. Lincoln was to deliver *a few appropriate remarks* at the dedication, following the lengthy main speech by Edward Everett of Massachusetts.

Four score and seven years ago our fathers brought forth on this continent a new nation, conceived in Liberty, and dedicated to the proposition that all men are created equal. Now we are engaged in a great civil war, testing whether that nation, or any nation, so conceived and so dedicated, can long endure. We are met on a great battle-field of that war. We have come to dedicate a portion of that field, as a final resting place for those who here gave their lives that that nation might live. It is altogether fitting and proper that we should do this. But, in a larger sense, we can not dedicate —we can not consecrate—we can not hallow—this ground. The brave men, living and dead, who struggled here, have consecrated it, far above our poor power to add or detract. The world will little note, nor long remember what we say here, but it can never forget what they did here. It is for us the living, rather, to be dedicated here to the unfinished work which they who fought here have thus far so nobly advanced. It is rather for us to be here dedicated to the great task remaining before us—that from these honored dead we take increased devotion to that cause for which they gave the last full measure of devotion—that we here highly resolve that these dead shall not have died in vain—that this nation, under God, shall have a new birth of freedom—and that government of the people, by the people, for the people, shall not perish from the earth. Abraham Lincoln

I WILL NOT BE
A NUMBER

Rain, mud, and blood marked the takeover of the Spangler farm on Blacksmith Shop Road in Gettysburg , Pennsylvania on July 1, 1863 as the battling Union and Confederate forces surging back and forth left many mangled bodies in their wake. George Spangler's farm became the main battlefield hospital, although every farm quartered some of the wounded. During the course of the three-day Battle of Gettysburg, more than 1800 Union soldiers and 100 Confederates would be treated at the Spangler Farm. Because of heavy rains the basements of those buildings that had them were flooded. Many of the wounded faced treatment and operations under the eaves of the Spangler's massive barn, with rainwater splashing them as it cascaded from the roof. Seven Union surgeons under the direction of Dr. Daniel G. Brinton of Chester, Pennsylvania tried desperately to keep up with the incoming wounded. Most serious wounds in limbs led to amputations using the same tools and cloths on multiple patients without any form of sterilization. Those with major head and body trauma were deemed mortally wounded and given only pain-killer treatments to ease their inevitable transition to death. This is the story of one such patient. We look in on him inside the barn on July 2ⁿᵈ, one day after he was shot during the first round of fighting. Doctors and assistants rush back and forth, trying to cope with the chaos around them. Our subject, an officer, talks with a private he has had brought to his bedside following that enlisted man's lower leg amputation.

Danforth, I've discovered an intriguing aspect of this process of dying; and the surgeon assures me that I have no hope of eluding death. My epiphany is that I am now living in the past, present and future, all at the same time. To be precise, I am in quite present agony because of the minié ball that pierced my left side and shattered to slice up my bowels. The doctor managed to clamp off the bleeding, but I'm oozing other fluids into my gut and none of my internal plumbing works anymore. I'm living in the past, because I actually am seeing various periods of my life as I prepare for death and I'm wondering how a Confederate soldier could have shot me in the left side as I stood behind the center of our ranks urging the men forward during the very first volley of this battle. One of our own men must have shot me, either accidentally or on purpose. The how and why don't really matter at this point. I'm afraid that in death I'll have a kinship with that graycoat, Stonewall Jackson, who was also shot by his own people at Chancellorsville a couple of months ago. He held off death for eight days. I doubt that I'll last that long. The battle here at Gettysburg is still raging, and I don't expect to outlive its hostilities by more than a day or two."

"Hey, Doc, it hurts pretty badly. Could you conjure up another one of those opium pills? … Better make it two. Thanks."

"Getting back to my living in other times, I feel like I'm in the future, because even though I'm closed up here in Spangler's barn, my mind sees acres of bodies of men and horses and gravestones. They're going to write books about the thousands on both sides who died here at Gettysburg, and I refuse to be one of their anonymous numbers. I'm drafting you to document that I've had a good life, Private Danforth. Your job will be to tell my story to others so that I won't be completely forgotten. I reckon that the closest thing people have to life after death is someone remembering them.

Yes, I realize that you have your own wound to worry about, but you'll get over that amputation below your left knee. They'll give you a wooden leg, and you'll go back to civilian life. I wish you the very best of futures. I'm picking on you to be the keeper of my memories because I've seen you writing long letters home. That tells me that you know how to handle the language and that you have caring people to share stories with. Both of those things suit my goals and portend a thriving life for you. Don't get me wrong; I'll see that you're paid for passing along my story. My brother Charlie is here with the Wisconsin Sharpshooters, and I'll ask him to take care of your needs.

As I said earlier, people are going to think of those dying here at Gettysburg as faceless numbers. You're going to remind them that I was a human being with a damned interesting life. Here we go; you should start writing now.

My full name is George Henry Stevens, although I'm known to most as George H. Stevens. I doubt that many know my middle name ... I'll try not to ramble so much. Between the pain and those pills, it's a little hard to think straight.

I guess I was one of the lucky ones, being born into a family of some means in New York City and later educated in private schools there. My birth date was December 8, 1831, just about thirty-one-and-a-half years ago. My parents were socially active, due to my father, John, being a shipping merchant. He and my mother, Lucy, were well regarded, both for their personalities and for Dad's ability to import hard-to-obtain commodities for the upper class folks. I was the fourth of five children and the only one who left New York looking for adventure and opportunity at an early age. Actually, my adventures started in New York City, following the Astor Place riot in 1849. I joined the 7th Regiment of the National Guard after seeing how well the militia handled the angry mob. Their acts of courage convinced me that there was something special about a military life, at least for a while. Without additional riots to put down, I became bored as a member of the Guard, and in 1852, at twenty-one years of age, I drew upon my father's shipping connections to secure a passage to Australia. I had always considered that a special place with great challenges and opportunities for young people.

Unfortunately, the real Australia didn't match my fantasies. Most of the country was completely undeveloped, and there were far too few women to satisfy the number of men there. I tried several business ventures in Australia, but none of them worked out. Romances didn't either. I finally gave up and returned to the States and New York in the summer of 1855. Fortunately, my old friends and contacts pointed me toward an opportunity in Milwaukee, going into the retail business with a local man named V. V. Livingston.

"Hey, Doc, that pill's wearing off. Get me another one when you get a chance."

As I was saying, I ended up working a business in Milwaukee, and in my spare time I took another crack at the military by joining the Second Company Light Guard. It was more of a fraternal group than a regiment, and I won a prize medal as the best drilled member. I was a sergeant then. The combination of military and merchant work led me to move to Fox Lake, Wisconsin in the fall of 1858, where I opened a grocery store and sent for my brother Charlie to help me run it."

"Double thanks, Doc; I won't take the second pill until I really need it. I have to keep my head clear while I tell Danforth my story. He's a good listener and writes well too."

"Things get slow in Fox Lake during the winter months, so I organized a voluntary military unit I called the Citizens Guard. It kept me interested in something beyond business. ... I shouldn't say that. I was involved at the Congregational Church, even though my parents had raised me Episcopalian. Through church contacts, I met Harriet Purdy and married her in 1859 on March 23rd. If she were here, she'd be pleased that I remember our wedding date.

Harriet and I had some good times together, despite the separations caused by my military obligations and the war. Our son Walter was born in February of 1860, and she's carrying a second child right now. I won't be around for him or her, but I hope Harriet raises that child to think well of me. You'll have to greet him or her for me, Danforth. I hope you can be like a godfather to my kids.

Anyway, in April of 1861, When President Lincoln

called for more troops to put down the rebellion, they gave me a commission as a captain and instructed me to reorganize my Citizens Guard unit and recruit more men for it. We met our requirement right away and marched to Camp Randall in Madison. There, we were renamed Company "A" of the Second Regiment Wisconsin Volunteer Infantry, and were the first unit to change our enlistment from three months to three years. They transported our regiment to Washington, D.C., and we saw our first action at the First Battle of Bull Run.

Following Bull Run, there were a whole string of battles, some with the 2nd Wisconsin acting alone, and later as part of the Iron Brigade, which included the 2nd, 6th, and 7th Wisconsin regiments plus regiments from Indiana and Michigan. At Second Bull Run, I ended up in command of the 2nd Wisconsin as a captain because of the loss of the colonel and the wounding of the lieutenant colonel. I missed the Antietam battle because of illness. – There was so much of that among the troops everywhere. I was a major, serving under Burnside at Fredericksburg, and a lieutenant colonel under Hooker at the Second Battle of Fredericksburg. We had a major skirmish with the enemy at Fitz-Hugh Crossing just prior to the Chancellorsville combat, but we weren't involved in the main event there.

Hold it for a minute, Danforth, while I take my reserve opium pill."

"You've been through so much, sir. I didn't join the Second Wisconsin until just after Second Fredericksburg. I was with you at that skirmish before Chancellorsville, and then got hit with you yesterday."

"Yes, yesterday was the capper, in several ways. You're done with soldiering and will go home to be with your family. I'm on my way out and will go home to God. I'll soon find out what He thinks of soldiers and our killing each other.... I started to say *old soldiers*, but I won't live to see my thirty-second birthday. The worst damn thing about yesterday isn't that we got hit during the first full-scale volley of this battle, but that the 2nd Wisconsin lost so many men. Doc told me that only 34 men were present for roll call on Cemetery Hill last night. We started the day with 306 men, 278 of whom were combatants. That's the number that fought in the morning to keep the Confederates, under Archer, from breaking through from McPherson Ridge to the heights on Cemetery Hill. We held them back, but due to the way we recruit units made up of neighbors, there are going to be many villages in Wisconsin without any young men left.

Believe it or not, Danforth, you're one of the lucky ones. These surgeons and self-trained medical people can save those wounded in their limbs through amputations, but a snowball in hell has a better chance of surviving than those of us who were hit in the head or the gut. Then there are all those who die from diseases before the battles even start. I wonder if men on the two sides of this war will ever be friends again.... God, this gut of mine hurts. The pills don't nearly free me from pain."

"I've taken seven pages of notes, sir. I think that's enough for now. You try to rest. As soon as there's a lull in the fighting, I'll send one of the assistants here to fetch your brother, Charlie. Sharpshooters don't fight after the sun sets, not that there is much sun getting through the battle smoke and frequent rainstorms. We'll get him here in time. I promise."

Lieutenant Colonel George H. Stevens succumbed on July 5, 1863, two days after the fighting at Gettysburg ceased. His remains were buried at Evergreen Cemetery in Gettysburg, with his family stating that they planned to take him back to Wisconsin after the war ended. Thanks to the dedication of a new National Cemetery adjacent to Evergreen on November 19, 1863, marked by Lincoln's Gettysburg Address, the Stevens family decided that he should permanently rest there. He is buried in a grave immediately behind and to the left of a large marker that reads WISCONSIN 73 BODIES.

Death did not end the story of George H. Stevens. At the Iron Brigade Reunion in 1887, a Clark County veteran said in an interview, "The first captain of Company A was George H. Stevens. He was killed as lieutenant colonel at the battle of Gettysburg. He was a splendid soldier (the only soldier so described)." Excerpting from *Reminiscences of the Battle of Gettysburg* by First Lieutenant Cornelius Wheeler, U.S.V. [Read April 5, 1893.]: Wheeler quotes Mr. H. J. Fahnestock, at that time a resident of Gettysburg, from his letter to Wheeler, "There is no question that the opening fight was between the two roads (the Fairfield and Chambersburg pikes) and spread later in the fight to the north, beyond the Chambersburg pike. The spot where [General] Reynolds is reported to have received his death-wound was at a copse of trees almost due west from the main seminary building, and about equidistant between the Fairfield road and the Chambersburg pike." Wheeler goes on to summarize, "This is where the Iron Brigade, the Second Wisconsin in advance, opened the battle of Gettysburg. [It is also where George H. Stevens received his mortal wound shortly after 10:30 a.m. on the morning of July 1, 1863.]"

From *Legend and Lore: Congregational Church, Fox Lake, WI*, "In the opening volley on the first day of the Battle of Gettysburg, Captain (sic) George Stevens was killed. Just a short stone toss away from him, Lucius Fairchild, future governor of Wisconsin, lost his arm. George Stevens was buried at Gettysburg, and his wife Harriet is buried in Riverside Cemetery here. After the war, Fox Lake veterans organized George H. Stevens Post 100 of the Grand Army of the Republic. Harriet Stevens presented a beautiful silk banner to them." (on May 18, 1886)

Harriet had paid fifty dollars to have the banner made for the George H. Stevens GAR Post No. 100. In 1930, the GAR was disbanded, and the banner was given to Lucy Hunter, the adult daughter of George Stevens. She had not yet been born when he died. Lucy decided to give the banner to the Fox Lake Public Library, where it was in a display case until the library moved to a new building in 1951. During the move someone at the library decided to discard the old GAR banner. A local veteran, Bill Linke, saw the banner on the garbage truck and rescued it. After an intervening period, Bill donated the banner to the Fox Lake American Legion Post. They held the banner in gradually declining condition until 1990, when they decided to raise funds to restore it as a valuable piece of history. The fundraising was completed in 2001 after some extra special events to achieve the necessary goal, and the restored banner was returned to Fox Lake, Wisconsin on Memorial Day in 2002. It was dedicated and enshrined in the American Legion Post during the 2002 Fox Lake Historical Days celebration.

Harriet's original cost for the banner had been $50. The cost for restoring it was $4595, and the display case for it cost $1475.

George H. Stevens: adventurer, businessman, and splendid soldier, achieved his goal. He lives on in the traditions of Fox Lake, Wisconsin. He is not an anonymous number in the statistics of Gettysburg.

PETER CONOVER HAINS, A SIGNIFICANT LIFE

In 1916, Major General Peter Conover Hains reflected on the progress of the war in Europe as he looked out his office window at the Potomac River and the Washington, DC scene. As Division Engineer for the Army Corps of Engineers, his recall to active duty from retirement had been an honor, freeing up a younger officer for duty in Europe. General Hains was not only a senior officer. At seventy-six, he was the oldest officer in the Army.

It had been a long arduous journey from his youth as the son of a struggling shoemaker in Philadelphia. Despite his poor background he had managed to secure entry into the U.S. Military Academy at West Point in 1857. He was in the first class that graduated in four years rather than the traditional five. When he was graduated from West Point in June of 1861, his classmates included two soon-to-be Generals, George Armstrong Custer of the Union Army and Pierce Manning Butler Young of the Confederate Army.

Commissioned Second Lieutenant in the 2nd U.S.

Artillery, Hains was given the honor of firing the first shot at the Battle of Bull Run. In 1862, he transferred to the Corps of Engineers and faced off against the Confederate enemy in thirty engagements. At Vicksburg, Mississippi, his commanding officer was too ill to participate, so Hains was assigned to General Grant's staff where he designed the siege plans for the Union Army 13th Corps. He received a brevet promotion to Major when Vicksburg was captured. (July 4, 1863 – one day after the conclusion of the Battle of Gettysburg in Pennsylvania)

In 1864, Peter Hains married Virginia Pettis Jenkins, daughter of Admiral Thornton Jenkins, Union Admiral Farragut's Chief of Staff. They had three sons, John Powers Hains, Peter Hains, and Thornton Jenkins Hains. John followed his father into a military career, achieving the rank of Colonel, Peter served as a Captain at Fort Hamilton in Brooklyn, and Thornton wrote popular novels and magazine stories about the sea.

Getting back to the military career of Peter Conover Hains, he served in the Spanish-American War in 1898 as a Brigadier General of volunteers. In 1903, he was promoted to Brigadier General in the Regular Army. He retired in 1904 at the mandatory retirement age of sixty-four, but with the outbreak of World War I, he was recalled to active duty as a Major General by special act of Congress. Hains was one of only two soldiers who served in the Civil War, the Spanish-American War, and World War I. The other individual was Charles King, four years younger, who served in the Army for seventy years from 1862 to 1932.

General Hains' personal career progressed steadily. The same could not be said for two of his three sons. While serving in the Philippines in 1907, Thirty-six year old Captain Peter Hains, the second oldest son, received tips from friends at home that his wife was unfaithful to him and having an affair with publisher William Annis. Once Peter returned home, he did his own investigating and gathered enough evidence to convince himself of his wife's infidelity. Peter decided the situation required action, and on August 15, 1908, he and his brother Thornton, who had a reputation for wild adventures, headed for Annis' yacht club in Bayside, New York. They were both armed and ready for action. While Thornton held back the crowd, including William Annis' wife, Peter shot Annis six times as he climbed off his sloop. Then the two brothers calmly sat down and waited for the police to arrive. Despite claiming Dementia Americana, the mental imbalance that supposedly strikes every American man when he finds his wife cheating on him, Peter was convicted and sentenced to serve time in Sing Sing prison. Thornton was acquitted, even though his defense took the previously untried stand that Dementia Americana was contagious, and he caught it from his brother. In 1911, General Hains persuaded the Governor of New York to pardon his son Peter. Rank does accumulate favors and political clout.

As indicated earlier, in 1862 during the Civil War, Lieutenant Peter C. Hains transferred from an artillery unit to the Corps of Engineers. For many, such a shift might have been made due to a whim. In Peter's case, he had a definite aptitude for engineering, although some of his later accomplishments may have resulted from on-the-job training.

In 1870 Peter Conover Hains was promoted to

the rank of Major and assigned as District Engineer for the Fifth District of the U.S. Lighthouse Service. He designed and was in charge of the construction of many lighthouses, including those at Morris Island, South Carolina and St. Augustine, Florida. Both of those lighthouses are still operational today, with the one in St. Augustine now functioning as a maritime museum as well.

Hains followed up his lighthouse engineering by being in charge of a huge project to rid the swampy DC area of its stench. Under his command, the Corps of Engineers dredged the Potomac and Anacastia Rivers. The dredged earth was used to raise adjacent swampy land and create new higher ground that is now known as East Potomac Park and Hains Point. Hains designed and built the Tidal Basin, the focus of the annual Cherry Blossom Festival plus Memorials to Thomas Jefferson, Martin Luther King, Jr., Franklin Delano Roosevelt, and George Mason. He next designed and built the "National Road" from Aqueduct Bridge to Mt. Vernon, which is now called the George Washington Parkway.

Peter C. Hains served on both the Nicaragua Canal Commission and the Panama Canal Commission during the period when the decision to build a canal had been made but dual routes were under consideration. He is credited with successfully convincing the other commission members to locate the canal in Panama.

Peter Conover Hains would have been historically significant, if only for his lengthy military career that spanned sixty-one years and three wars. Add to that his design and construction of lighthouses that still function today, major engineering landmarks and innovations in the District of Columbia area, plus winning arguments deciding the location and route for the Panama Canal, and you justify calling his life historically significant indeed.

COFFEE 9/29/2021 (NATIONAL COFFEE DAY)

My first instance of "imbibing" coffee had nothing to do with the liquid. Boston's old Kennedy Butter and Eggs stores featured open sacks of different varieties of coffee beans. When I was shopping with my mother, I would pick up an individual bean and chew it. Sometimes, I would chew individual beans from two or more sacks to discover the differences in taste among them.

For many years, Mom barred me from drinking liquid coffee on the grounds [sic] that it would stunt my growth. When I was in the seventh grade, she finally allowed me to pour a small amount of coffee into my milk and add a teaspoonful of sugar. It was sweet, weak, highly milk-diluted iced coffee. Speaking of iced coffee, it was standard practice in Massachusetts diners and restaurants to pour all the end-of-day coffee into a cold drink dispenser for use as iced coffee on subsequent days. My breakthrough with coffee came when I was in the eighth grade and my friend, Sam Oxman, recruited me to work concessions as part of his father's crew at the stock car races at Norwood Arena in Norwood, Massachusetts. The term, stock car races, was a misnomer. All the cars were a minimum of ten years old, and while they had races, the drivers were as much interested in smashing their opponents' cars as they were in winning the race. Because many of the cars had survived multiple collisions, there was a definite element of danger that wheels and other parts of vehicles would fly up into the grandstands. All the races took place in the evening, when it was chilly, bordering on freezing. The only cure for the cold I had as a wandering vendor in the grandstand and at the entrance gates was to periodically visit the food concession booth for black coffee. Cream and sugar might have sufficed for a single cup, but I needed to drink the hot brew repeatedly, all evening long. At first, it tasted bitter and strange, but given the need to withstand the cold, black coffee soon became my elixir of life. From that time forward, I drank my coffee black, cherishing the taste of the beans rather than added condiments. My one exception to this rule was the addition of a bit of bourbon when I wasn't feeling well.

Once I started writing, I projected my love of coffee onto some of my characters. In my Lord's Prayer and Imp mystery series, my lead investigator, Pastor Arthur Blake, consumes coffee almost as a religious sacrament. In one novel, he even reflects my past with his tale of once having worked at stock car races in Wisconsin. In *Loyalties*, Todd Weatherford and all his associates in the Bahamas have coffee as a major ingredient for every meeting or social event. In my first science fiction novel, Mac Blackwell is elated when he discovers there is a variety of coffee in Hallywalooly.

In many instances, coffee is a convenient prop to allow

a character to indulge while musing over his or her problems. In other cases, it is a social device to increase comfort between strangers meeting for the first time or facing a common problem. For me, it is a source of satisfaction and a catalyst for composing my thoughts. It has many values for those who appreciate it.

CELEBRITY AIN'T FOR ME

I'm no Stephen King or Tom Clancy. I've been writing novels and self-help books for twelve years, twelve books plus a bunch of miscellany, all with modest readership, but aspects of celebrity never touched me, until last Thursday.

At my writers' workshop, I absorbed wisdom from a well-known author and teacher on the subject of revision, washed down by multiple cups of black coffee. When the speaker paused for the traditional ten-minute break, I made a beeline for the men's room and the nearest urinal. As the process began, someone stepped up to the urinal next to mine. Adhering to the code of privacy, I didn't glance at him.

Suddenly, a voice said, "You've written a series of mysteries?"

Forced to respond I said, "Actually, two series."

"Private detective?"

"An amateur sleuth. He's a pastor who earlier was a NASA engineer, and now he's doing more and more investigating."

"Are your books historical?"

"They all show how things that happened in the past affect the present."

"Is the crime in the past?"

"Not usually. The detective work takes place in the present."

This time the voice came from behind me. "Then they're not like Brother Cadfael?"

"No."

"Thanks."

I heard the men's room door open and close. I reached for the flush lever and mentally shook my head. I'd had my first celebrity author interview, and I hadn't liked it one bit. How could celebrities put up with well-meaning but constant invasions of their privacy? I now could understand why many wear disguises when they go out in public.

I washed my hands and figuratively washed them free of celebrity. Celebrity sells books, but it has its downside too.

TRICK OR TREAT

It was 1944. At the age of six, I thought World War II was a normal part of life. It had been going on for as long as I could remember, and I assumed that someday, I would grow up and become part of it. We (my mother, my older sister, and I) lived in Brighton, Massachusetts, part of Boston, in an apartment house on busy Commonwealth Avenue. Even though the war was oceans away from us in two directions, we felt that we were part of it.

One of my earliest recollections, at three years old, had been of the day my mother took me down to Harvard Avenue in early December to buy my first snow shovel. The one she picked out had a red blade and was just the right size for me. As Mom and I stood on the street corner waiting for the traffic light to change, I held her hand tightly with my left hand and gripped my new shovel just as firmly with my right. Suddenly, a man I didn't know ran up and shouted to us and to anyone else nearby who would listen, "The Japs have bombed Pearl Harbor!"

I heard several adults around me ask, "Where's Pearl Harbor?" I think some of them wondered if it was somewhere near us on the New England coastline.

Over the course of the next three years, we learned that the war would make changes in everyone's life. We discovered ration books and stamps that we could use or trade for something we wanted with a higher priority;

saving metal foil gum and other wrappers and rolling them into balls; and pouring hot cooking fat into cans for conversion into munitions in some mysterious way. We made sure every evening that our window shades didn't let any light escape, and we listened for air raid sirens and took part in drills. My uncle's bedding factory converted to making inflatable rafts and stocking them with emergency supplies like c-rations and signaling mirrors. When my aunt and uncle drove us to visit my mother's parents on Sundays, we drove past MIT, where I stared in fascination at the sentries with rifles pacing back and forth in front of a building on Memorial Drive.

At the Saturday afternoon movie matinees, the newsreels became just as important as the double feature, and *Life Magazine* required instant study as soon as it arrived, whether in the morning or the afternoon mail delivery.

As soon as I reached school age, I saved my pennies for stamps that we pasted into books to buy War Bonds, and classroom geography and history studies centered on the locations of current battles and the many countries that had joined into present and past conflicts. The loyalties of the various countries also became my focus as I started to collect postage stamps from around the world.

With friends and my sister, we tried to plant a Victory Garden in the back yard of our apartment house, but we had little success penetrating the packed-down stony earth that didn't even allow blades of grass to survive in the shadows of the surrounding buildings.

Our finest war support venture came at the suggestion of my friend Bobby's father. Ed Newman was one of the last of a disappearing breed. He worked as a hat blocker, but in his spare time, he served as a Cub Scout Leader. Ed pointed out to us that Halloween would soon be upon us, and that we could use the traditional Trick or Treat ritual for patriotic purposes.

The focus of our effort would be the Marine Hospital that was located on Warren Street, about eight blocks from our apartment house. Marines injured in fighting around the world, ended up in Brighton for surgery and rehabilitation.

The key to our campaign's success was that we two friends (I was six years old, and Bobby was seven.) would go Trick or Treating on the evening before Halloween, avoiding competition from other kids. We canvassed four apartment buildings, announcing to each surprised tenant: "Trick or Treat for the Marine Hospital". We asked them only for magazines and comic books, because we knew that the Marines would be in the hospital for a long time and needed reading materials. Television was a thing of the future, and those endless hours in the hospital seemed to be even longer than they seem today. Bobby and I contributed a substantial number of our personal comic books, many of which would be worth an amazing amount of money today.

Our efforts were more successful than we thought possible. The following afternoon, on Halloween, 1944, Bobby and I each walked into the lobby of the Marine Hospital with a loaded red wagon full of magazines and comic books, and Bobby's father, Ed, trailed us with a larger cart full of similar reading materials. The uniformed Marine at the front desk showed surprise on his face when our cart convoy arrived, and he thanked us enthusiastically.

In terms of the total war effort, our bit of logistical support was insignificant, but it showed at least a few Marines that even small children appreciated their sacrifices.

SALUTE TO VETERANS ON PARADE

I lost a friend the other day;

Won't see him anymore.

There were many other friends

That I had lost before.

Way back in the Forties

They signed up for a War,

And went to many places

Unknown to them before.

Those who made it back rejoiced

Family life would be in store.

Old age would let them finally tell

What happened in that War.

In recent years they marched again

Parading each July Four

Wearing uniforms that didn't fit,

Smelling of mothballs from the store.

First they marched.

Then they rode.

Now, they ride no more.

First they marched.

Then they rode.

Now, they ride no more.

FAREWELL TO A HERO – GALE SAYERS

Sep 23, 2020, 5:54 PM

Graceful beyond belief as he ran

Able to elude multiple potential tacklers

Level-headed and modest, if not shy

Entering football's Hall of Fame at just 34 years old

Scoring six touchdowns in a single game

Always running like poetry in motion

Yielding to a knee injury that ended his playing days

Eager to share his awards with cancer-stricken Brian Piccolo

Running an office supply business with his wife after

football

Said to be the smoothest runner he had ever seen by George Halas

Legendary Bears coach George Halas, as he presented Sayers for his Hall of Fame induction, said, "If you want to see perfection as a running back, you best get ahold of a film of Gale Sayers. He was poetry in motion. His like will never be seen again."

Gale wrote his autobiography, *I am Third* upon which the movie Brian's Song was based. ("God is first. My friends are second. I am third.")

For the final years of his life, Gale battled Alzheimer's Disease.
Upon his death, his brother lamented that Gale had so many wonderful memories, and all of a sudden they were gone.

Gale and his wife Ardith attended our church for several years, although Ardith came every week while Gale came infrequently because he received too much attention as a celebrity. I had several chances to have conversations with him. He was most at ease when we stayed off the subject of football and talked about our two small businesses and the problems we encountered in keeping them going.

We had church auctions for fund-raising, and Gale contributed a signed football. After the lively bidding went to more than $500 before being closed, Gale went to his car trunk and signed two more footballs so that the second and third bidders could have one also, at the same price, thus raising more than $1000 extra for the church.

He was more than a great football player. He was a great man. His football career and his fully functional life were cut much too short.

Many of us will miss him.

HOUSE CALLS

When I was a child (a long time ago in a galaxy far, far away), a cold, stomach ache, or childhood contagious disease would prompt a telephone call to the doctor, following which he would come to our apartment to examine me. In Massachusetts at that time, doctors had M.D. emblems attached to their license plates and emergency house call cards to put on their dashboards to avoid parking tickets.

We had only one doctor, whether the illness call was for me, my older sister, or my mother. The concept of specialists didn't apply to us. A cold would trigger advice like "Take two aspirin, drink plenty of fluids, and call me in the morning." A stomach ache often included advice to "Drink ginger ale. The ginger in it will calm your stomach." If I had one of the major childhood diseases, I hit the jackpot. "Aspirins, fluids, bed rest, and stay home from school for two weeks."

Despite the extra time and energy involved in making house calls, doctor bills were relatively inexpensive in those days. They increased dramatically with the advent of private health insurance at the beginning of the 1950s decade and pressure by insurance companies and unions to force employers to provide insurance as a fringe benefit of employment. A large customer base was required to allow private insurers to control the health system. Establishment of that base encouraged greater medical specialization by doctors and expansion of hospital facilities. It also virtually eliminated house calls because patients with insurance who once treated themselves with home remedies soon felt free to consult expensive specialists for minor ailments. In 1930, 40% of a doctor's appointments were house calls. By 1972, house calls had decreased to 5% of those appointments, and by 1980, the percentage was only 1%. Doctors stayed in their offices and treated patients on an assembly line basis, with nurses and assistants handling all parts of the process except for direct medical consultations.

In recent years, there has been a resurgence of house calls in several different formats.

The COVID-19 pandemic disrupted medical services procedures. Entire hospitals were dedicated to pandemic patient treatments only. Individual patients skipped their periodic doctor visits for fear of leaving home and catching COVID during the process. For the first time in many years, medical practices were losing money, finding staff difficult to maintain, and being forced to delay optional patient procedures. To offset the reductions in patient care, health organizations approved telephone and remote video appointments, a step that had previously been treated as inadequate and unprofessional. This procedure compensated for many of the missed in-person appointments and suited the pandemic needs to avoid unnecessary travel and crowds. It had the unforeseen benefits of easing access to popular specialists and decreasing traffic in emergency rooms.

Even before the COVID-19 pandemic struck, some medical companies and healthcare systems had initiated concierge medicine, an approach where the patient pays a monthly or annual fee for prompt access to doctors, whether by in-office visit, house call, or telephone/video link. Concierge medicine is sometimes labeled boutique medicine, reflecting the high fees charged on a subscription basis for guaranteed access to doctors without a long wait for an available appointment.

A few medical companies have actively returned to the house call format. A typical company of this type recruits a staff of doctors who are willing to be on call twelve hours per day, but only work sixteen days per month. This workload attracts doctors with outside interests because they have two weeks every month of free time. The age distribution of patients for this typical house call company is bimodal with statistical peaks for numbers of patients at one year and 36 years of age. They do, of course, care for older patients, with the oldest so far being 103, but surprisingly, the elderly are not a major part of their business, perhaps because Medicare may not favor this model. When one of these doctors makes a house call, he or she is driven by a trained person who organizes the required medical equipment, assists the doctor with procedures, and protects the doctor from physical confrontations and unfounded scandalous complaints.

Another format for the return of the house call is the ability of a primary care or other physician to requisition in-home care on a scheduled visit basis from organizations that specialize in such services. Typical requisitioned services are physical and occupational therapy plus nursing care for a specified condition. Medicare covers a limited number of such visits, but the guiding rule is the physician's decision on medical necessity.

Medical house calls in various formats are available once again. They are much more expensive than the old-fashioned kind, their costs hidden from the patient by insurance company and Medicare guidelines. Even in the situation where the in-house care-giver is a physician rather than an assistant, the specific doctor will vary depending on work assignment schedules. As with many commodities, you pay more and receive something less than the original. However, something is still better than nothing.

PART THREE - EXCERPTS

HUNGARIAN GOLD TRAIN

(Excerpt from *Lead Us Not into Temptation*)

He had been Captain John Hendrix then, stationed in Salzburg, Austria in 1946 following the war. His job as liaison to the United Nations had been to assist the UN to reunite displaced persons with other surviving members of their families. His work involved cross-tabulating all available census records for the different camps. This job put him into contact with those who were trying to reunite art treasures and valuables stolen by the Nazis with their original owners. He had become especially friendly with some of the enlisted men and officers of the 5th Infantry Regiment. Their duties included guarding the huge Property Control Warehouse in Salzburg.

The Property Control Warehouse contained all manner of valuable items accumulated by the German Army from the homes of Jewish families, museums in conquered territories, and executed prisoners in the concentration camps. It also contained property confiscated by the American Army from Nazi leaders and German aristocrats at the end of the war. By far the biggest source of the treasure in the warehouse was the Hungarian Gold Train. The advancing American forces captured this train in Werfen, Austria on May

16, 1945. The train had been loaded with gold, jewelry, art, and other valuables seized from the Hungarian Jewish population as well as some museum treasures. The pro-Nazi Hungarian government had developed the treasure train project in an attempt to keep their confiscated riches and museum treasures away from the rapidly advancing Soviet forces. They were attempting to reach neutral Switzerland after months of gathering additional voluntary and compulsory contributions and fighting off robbery attempts by both German SS and Nazi-Hungarian troops. The advancing American Army discovered the train partially concealed in the Tauern Tunnel south of Salzburg, Austria. It had been stopped there in an attempt to evade allied bombers. The Americans took the captured train to Werfen where its contents were unloaded and then transferred to the Property Control Warehouse in Salzburg.

The Property Control Warehouse had tight security, but it soon became apparent that many of the valuables were going right out the front door. Generals and others of high rank were requisitioning unique and irreplaceable items to furnish their offices and those of headquarters associates. This became obvious to the troops assigned to guard the warehouse, and before long there were frequent clandestine visits to the warehouse by enlisted personnel who removed items and sometimes shared them with the guards.

Captain John Hendrix found himself in the position of having accumulated priceless valuables both through high-level associates who had simply requisitioned them for his use and through friends in the security regiment who had *liberated* them. These acquisitions of priceless items had seemed so unreal to him that he had little trouble reacting to them as being outside the realm of right versus wrong. He and his friends had simply convinced themselves that they were entitled to them because of all they had suffered during their wartime service.

OMAHA BEACH

(Nonfiction excerpt from *Give Us this Day Our Daily Bread* related by fictional character)

I was a Pharmacist's Mate in the Sixth Naval Beach Battalion, a unit that was assembled and trained under hush-hush conditions. The reason for all the security was that our mission was to be among the first to land whenever and wherever the Allies invaded mainland Europe. We were trained to support the assault troops with medical aid, communications, and boat repair. We were also trained in the use of all kinds of weapons and were to serve as the traffic cops on the beach for landing troops safely with all of their support equipment and for evacuating the wounded. The invasion was a deep dark secret, so we were too. We trained for about fourteen months in the States, and then we were shipped to England a few months before D- Day. They put us under the command of the Army's 6th Engineer Special Brigade. We were sailors dressed like soldiers except that we wore black T-shirts under our field jackets, and our helmets had a blue/gray band around them and a red rainbow on the front.

The code name for the invasion of Normandy, France was Operation Overlord, and despite terrible weather that almost required a cancellation and limited the use of air power, the landings began on June 6, 1944. We were among the first headed for shore between 0600 and 0630 in the Easy Red sector of Omaha Beach. We were right behind the demolition teams that landed in inflated boats to try to clear some of the obstacles and mines that the Germans had set up. One set of obstacles was a series of telephone poles set into the beach angled toward the sea. They had mines mounted on their top ends set to detonate on impact by a landing craft or other vessel. The Germans discovered the demolition teams at work and threw everything they had at them. Those poor guys suffered about seventy percent losses, and there was no one else yet ashore to help them.

Our final approach to the beach was by LCI(L). That was the designation for a Landing Craft, Infantry (Large). It was about half the length of a football field with a ramp on each side of the bow that could be lowered to discharge troops and equipment. They were manned by Coast Guard crews.

One of the other landing craft, LCI(L)-85, that came in a bit after ours at 0735 was hit twenty-five times and later sank. Only six people got off its ramps unscathed. One of them was a friend of mine who told me later how, after a couple of the artillery hits, he had to take the fire hose and wash clusters of small body parts overboard. That violated all of his medical training, but it had to be done.

By comparison, we were lucky. Our LCI(L) got off course because of the weather. We reached shore about four hundred yards east of our designated landing spot. Because of this, we came in under a cliff where the Germans couldn't target us with their guns. We didn't quite make impact with the beach, and the water was very choppy, so three of us had to swim for shore with a heavy line. We secured it to one of those tilted telephone poles that had a mine on the top end, and our men had to wade through the surf with full packs of equipment by clinging to that line. In most cases the water was up to their armpits. Most of our people made it safely to shore even though we had incoming fire from anti-tank guns and machine guns. We did lose a lot of equipment when the waves knocked people over, and only two of our radios were working when we reached the shore.

For about six or seven hours we were pinned down at the high water mark where the beach sloped down at about forty-five degrees into the water. This area was covered with large water-smoothed multi-colored pebbles ranging from the size of a chicken egg to about four inches diameter. Whenever an artillery shell came close to us and hit in this area, the stones would start flying at high velocity. More of our people were wounded or killed by the flying stones than by the artillery shells.

Only one tank made it safely to shore in our area. He set himself up on that slope of pebbles, and moved forward up the slope each time he wanted to fire on the German positions. Then he backed down the slope to hide from incoming fire. We thought we would be safest hiding behind the tank, but we soon realized that he was drawing a lot of fire, and we moved away from him.

As more and more troops and equipment made it to the shore, the Germans stopped pinning us down because they had more important targets elsewhere. Then we started to do our best to tend to the wounded and get people ready for evacuation. Along the way, we saw two of our people crouched behind a half-track vehicle for shelter. A German shell hit the vehicle, lifted it into the air and dropped it on one of them. He died instantly.

During the initial bedlam of that first day, we were so tired and the wounded had been hit so badly that all we could do was give most of them morphine shots to ease their pain. At one point a buddy and I found our battalion commander lying on the beach with an unexploded shell in his shoulder. It had entered his body through his right collarbone and now protruded through his left shoulder blade. We managed to flag down a truck and took him to one of the few field hospitals that had been set up. Only the use of penicillin, which was a new breakthrough, saved his life.

Incoming Landing Craft and other ships were being hit by artillery and machinegun fire. Because of this they frequently discharged their troops too far from shore for them to wade in. A very small number of men who tried to swim the rest of the way managed to get ashore safely. Those who did only made it by discarding their heavy packs. Most drowned, and we fished as many bodies as possible out of the water. We had to drag the bodies beyond the high water mark to be sure that they wouldn't be reclaimed by the sea at high tide. This meant dragging the bodies beyond any hope of cover, directly toward the German guns.

During the early hours of the invasion I saw one soldier frantically signaling to me for help by waving the arm he had lost. Another had his leg blown off, and in his shock, he crawled to get it back in the apparent hope that somehow he would walk again. We found our Beachmaster lying shell-shocked next to boxes of burning hand grenades, but managed to get the boxes away from him before they exploded.

The original plans called for the landing craft to evacuate the wounded on their way back out to sea, so that no craft left empty. Because of the heavy German bombardment of incoming vessels during the first couple of days, the ships were ordered away from the beaches for safety without taking on any wounded, and we ended up having to care for large numbers of wounded for a lot longer than expected.

There were so many killed during the first day that we had to move the bodies with a bulldozer. We did this, both to keep the dead out of sight so they didn't demoralize the fresh assault troops as they landed on the beach, and also to clear a path for the new troops to follow toward the German gun emplacements. The infantry finally managed to clear the extension of that path of mines, and they climbed up a ravine to get to the top of the cliff. Then they circled behind the German beach defenses which were all aimed toward the sea. Most of the Germans surrendered without resistance, and the troops were able to move inland off the beach.

We didn't join them. Our job was to handle the evacuation of the wounded and to direct traffic inbound and outbound from the beach. I was on that bloody beach nineteen days before I was evacuated back to England.

For years afterward, I saw those beach landings and all the accompanying bloodshed in my dreams. I survived in some of those dreams, and in others I had a painful lingering death. That's why I've refused to talk about it until now. I didn't want to rouse my demons...

THE SMOKING TABLE

(Excerpt from *Forgive Us Our Trespasses*)

The coffee-time chatter faded away as they turned two corners on their way to the pastor's office. Arthur left the door open in anticipation of Irma's arrival. He gestured for Peter to sit at the conference table and then turned to get a mug of coffee from his personal pot before joining him. As Arthur sat down, Irma entered and, seeing his signal, closed the door behind her.

"Hello, Peter, it has been quite a while since you last visited us. It's great to see you again."

"Hi, Irma, I asked Arthur to invite you to this confab, because I trust your viewpoint and your discretion."

Irma heard the tension in Peter's tone and sat down, prepared for something significant and serious.

Arthur broke the silence. "Dad, why don't you start at the beginning? When I saw your expression in the congregation, I knew something was bothering you. Take a deep breath, and tell us about it."

Peter arched his back and stretched his legs as he leaned back in his chair. "You're right as usual, Arthur. Something is tearing me apart, and I don't know how to handle it.

"Irma, the background for my problem is the recent

death of my best friend. Albert Dandrich and I go way back together. We've been fishing buddies and hobbyists in local archeology and even partners in the county horseshoe tournaments. We've spent vacations together along with our wives, touring as a foursome all over the country. We even dragged Arthur along on some of those trips. I was really close to him, and his sudden death in an automobile accident was a shock."

"Was he your age?"

"No, Irma, he was quite a bit older...I'd guess that he was in his low eighties, but he was vigorous, and most people thought he was much younger."

"Dad, it's always a shock when a close friend dies, but there must be more to the story, or you wouldn't be here seeking our help and wanting to keep Mother from knowing about it."

"You're right, Arthur. The problem developed when Al's wife, Mandy, gave me his antique smoking table as a memorial keepsake. Al hadn't smoked for years, but he cherished that table and kept it next to his desk. He still had some old pipes and pouches of tobacco inside it. As soon as it arrived, Janice told me that I would have to clean it up in the garage and get rid of the remaining mixture of smells if I wanted to keep it in the house."

"Were you able to deodorize it completely?"

"I came close to that goal, Irma, and Janice even let me move it to our basement for further work, but that effort became less important when I discovered a secret compartment in the back of the pipe storage cabinet section. Lots of pieces of antique furniture have secret compartments, but this one was particularly well hidden. Being a lover of antiques, I was impressed by the craftsmanship that made the extra space behind the cabinet wall so difficult to detect. I was amazed to find that the craftsman had been able to match the wood grains on the inner and outer carved walls. The grains looked identical from both sides. Anyway, when I examined the contents of that cavity, I found some disturbing papers and other items that are the reason for my coming."

"It sounds as though you found a skeleton in Al's closet, Dad."

Peter shifted in his seat and stared at his son. "I wish you hadn't chosen those particular words, Arthur, because they are exactly correct. I found an old photograph of Al in a Nazi SS uniform complete with the grinning skull and bones insignia. There were even two embroidered skull badges in a small envelope. Penciled on the back of the photograph was the inscription *Obersturmfuhrer Wilhelm Schnacht*. I looked up the rank, and it would be the equivalent of a First Lieutenant. My best friend was a Nazi officer during World War II. I sat and stared at what I'd discovered for about an hour before I forced myself to believe it."

Irma reached over and touched Peter on the shoulder. "Are you absolutely sure that it was Albert in the picture and that he wasn't simply collecting war relics?"

Peter straightened up from his hunched position. His eyes squinted as he glared at them. His voice grew louder despite his clenched teeth. "It was Albert, all right. He had the same small scar on his right cheek, and he held his chin thrust out with pride. I've been best friends for decades with a war criminal. He wasn't an ordinary German soldier; he was an officer in the Waffen SS. He must have had all kinds of blood on his hands."

Peter's appearance softened again, and he sagged

back down in his chair. "Arthur, I've considered Albert and Mandy friends for longer than you've been alive. I don't know what to do about this."

FAMILY REQUEST

(Chapter One from *Thy Will Be Done*)

At the point in the service normally reserved for the closing benediction, Pastor Arthur Blake asked the congregation to be seated for a special message. He then relinquished the pulpit to a first-time visitor to Parkville United Methodist Church.

A blond muscular man with weightlifter shoulders flaring into his neck adjusted the microphone for his greater height. "Good morning. I want to thank Pastor Blake for giving me the opportunity to address you. I'm Ted Karga. My sister, Kristina Karga, worshipped with you for the last six months or so, until she died last week. The doctors still don't know why she left us so suddenly. She was only thirty-two years old."

Several people shook their heads and murmured comments to each other.

"I'm here this morning to ask if any of you may have borrowed or know the whereabouts of Kristina's journals. She maintained those journals for several years, and none of her friends know where to look for them. I need to learn why she died, and I'm hoping that her written entries will reveal key information. If you find the journals, please give them to Pastor Blake; he will get them to me.

"I apologize in advance for what I am about to say. My upbringing makes me tremble, but I can't hold it back anymore. … God, why did you make her die so young? She had so much to offer you and the world. I stand here in your house in front of your people, and I declare that you are not a God of love. She served you well, but I will no longer be one of your followers! You are no longer my God!" Ted screamed this last declaration and blinked back tears as he ran down the aisle and out of the church.

Pastor Blake prayed in response to Ted's outburst: *Forgive him, Lord; he can't really mean that.*

The buzz of reactive comments filled the sanctuary. A scattering of worshippers stood and stared at each other and the exit door. Wally Sanborn hastened out, trying to catch up with Ted. Some people stayed in their pews, but others moved around to talk with their friends. A few left the sanctuary in Wally's wake in an effort to keep Ted from breaking his religious connections.

After a long pause, Arthur stood and approached the pulpit as though drawn to it by a magnet. "If we ever needed a benediction, we need one now. … Lord, your ways are mysterious and difficult for us to accept at times like these. Be with Ted as he struggles with the loss of his only sister. Be with all of us now and in the future as we face our own losses and pain. We know that frustrated people may turn their backs on you, but you will not forsake them. Cherish your troubled children, all of us. And now, friends, go from this place, and seek God's meaning in your lives. He will be with you, even in terrible times. Amen.

Hesitantly and sporadically, individuals stood and moved slowly toward the exits. Most of the older ones left silently, while the chatter of the younger congregants displayed interest and even excitement.

DRIFTERS

(Chapter 16 from *Deliver Us from Evil*)

Their so-called office was the back room of Winoski's Tavern. Stan Winoski let them use it and occasionally sleep there for fifteen percent of their take. George Felkis, better known as *Feckless*, sat at a card table counting paper money and change he had emptied from ten plastic grocery bags. He wrote a total on a sticky-note pad and yelled over to *Grumpy* Horrigan, "We did better than yesterday. We ended up with one hundred eighty-seven dollars and sixty-three cents. That's close to thirty-five dollars per church. We could have had more if so many people didn't donate by checks. How did we do on the stuff they gave us? Can we sell much of it?"

Grumpy reached over to a pile of clothing and retrieved a brown tweed sport jacket. "The only good stuff today was clothing. We can usually get about ten dollars for a suit and five dollars for a sport jacket, but this tweed jacket should be worth more. I think it's your size if you want to keep it. I figure we can make about sixty dollars by selling the rest of the clothes and the other junk."

Feckless said, "Yeah, I'll try that coat. It'll be good for when we go to the racetrack. With your stuff, we pulled in close to two hundred and fifty dollars. If we could do that every day, we'd be golden. The trouble is that we have to keep moving to new areas so that we don't hit the same church more than once a year. Maybe we should go to veterans' halls and talk up our military backgrounds while we look for contributions."

"Just be sure to avoid talking about our being kicked out of the Army for going AWOL and then getting picked up by the police in a drug raid."

"We'd just say that we got out but couldn't land jobs because of psychological problems. That's almost the truth."

"We couldn't get jobs because we don't like to work hard."

"Grumpy, not liking to work or stick to a schedule is a psychological problem. Anyway, this jacket fits me pretty well. There are some papers in the inside pocket. I hope they're worth something."

"Are they stocks or bonds?"

Feckless opened the envelope and examined the papers. Then he gave out a low whistle. "These may be worth as much as stocks and bonds. The envelope's marked for someone named Charles King in one of those small towns we hit today. This must have been his jacket. Anyway, the envelope contains birth certificates for six different people. They look genuine."

"How are they worth money?"

"I have a strong feeling that if we contact this King guy, he's going to want to buy them back."

OLD HOUSES

(Chapter 7 from *Implications*)

For their house-hunting trip to Amboy, Irma drove her black Mustang, which she considered her almost-living pet. Arthur enjoyed the opportunity to relax and absorb the scenery as passenger instead of driver. He noticed many signs and buildings that hadn't registered in his consciousness when he had previously driven the same route. The online material they had studied about Amboy indicated that the village dated back to 1852, so they looked forward to seeing a fair number of houses from the late nineteenth and early twentieth centuries.

Because they wanted to familiarize themselves with Amboy, Arthur and Irma decided they would simply drive the streets and neighborhoods, stopping at houses bearing For Sale signs when they appeared interesting. They saw several interesting older houses, usually of frame construction and quite spacious due to their several additions over the years. However, it didn't take them long to realize that their dream of a home that was a hundred or more years old came with a flaw they hadn't anticipated. There were many such homes, and some of them were for sale, but none of them had the kind of location they wanted.

During the early days of Amboy, and most other Midwest villages, settlers had built their homes in a cluster, within easy walking distance of each other to encourage mutual support. As the village expanded, the older area became its downtown district. Subsequent razing of those homes that were in poor condition or in key locations led to construction of stores, schools, and small industrial shops within one or a few blocks of the older homes that survived. The Blakes found some still-elegant Victorian homes from the late nineteenth century, but those homes all lacked the charm of a relatively isolated neighborhood. The house described as having a stream on the property turned out to be in the business district and adjacent to railroad tracks used exclusively for freight trains.

Arthur had just suggested to Irma that they look farther out of town, perhaps at farmhouses, when his cell phone rang.

"Hello, this is Pastor Arthur Blake speaking."

"Hi, Arthur, it's Lorna Dyner. You may want to come back to our church site in Amboy. The state arson investigators found something very disturbing. It turns out that our church had a sub-basement that I never knew about. Perhaps the builders intended it to be a tornado shelter. Anyway, over the years everyone forgot about it. The investigators found a trap door leading to the sub-basement this morning and just came up after exploring it."

"We're actually in Amboy right now, so there's no problem about coming to your church. Is there something unusual about this sub-basement?"

"I'd call it unusual. They told me they found three bodies in there."

ALL AT ONCE

(Excerpt from *Impulses*)

"Pastor Blake, this is Annie at Bishop Chandler's office. Howard wanted to catch you before you left on a trip or committed to a project. We've just learned that Pastor Rebecca Klingham, who succeeded you at Parkville UMC, has committed suicide. We don't have any details for you. Bishop Chandler would like you to investigate the circumstances and deal with the police there. He'd also like you to substitute at that church for a few weeks until he is able to arrange for a full-time replacement. Thank you in advance for filling this void. Please call me if you have any questions."

Arthur made a few notes and pressed the button for the second message. "Hi, Arthur – Wally Sanborn here. Our young friend, Jeremy Hadley, apparently decided to look into the disappearance of a roommate, and now he's gone missing too. I've just learned this from his mother, Shirley. She's calm on the surface, but I know she's really upset inside. I'll be trying to determine the circumstances of Jeremy's disappearance. Call me when you can. We'll need your help."

Arthur made some more notes. Shirley Hadley had been his secretary at Parkville United Methodist Church. Wally Sanborn, the Lay Leader and a retired Army officer, was his coffee buddy and one of his best friends. The missing twenty-two year old Jeremy Hadley had assisted Arthur and Irma in several investigations.

He pushed the button for the third message on the answering machine. "Hello, Arthur, this is Mother calling. Your father and I have to go to California because his cousin Ralph has been in a bad automobile accident. Ralph has no other living relatives. We need to ask you and Irma to manage the antiques store while we're gone. Call us as soon as possible. We're booking our flight now."

A few notes and a few sips of coffee later, Arthur returned to the back yard. "Irma, you may not believe this, but our lack of projects is no longer a problem. Our calendar has overflowed."

"As soon as you came out of the door, I knew that you felt happier. You can't function when things are going well. Dreams or no dreams, you thrive when surrounded by people seeking solutions to their problems."

A LONG TIME AGO

(Excerpt from *Impostor*)

The driver of the long black Jaguar would not respond to his questions about their destination or the identity of the person who had requested a meeting with him. When they exited his flat, they encountered an excited mob of neighbors surrounding the new 1936 limousine. The crowd circulated around the vehicle examining the large headlights and wing-mounted spare tires, while peering through the windscreen to see the interior. The chauffeur's authoritative bearing parted the onlookers, as he guided his passenger to the rear door. Upon entering the vehicle, the passenger admitted to himself that the car equally impressed him. This whole scene was out of kilter.

Why would anyone with a limousine and a uniformed chauffeur even know about him? He was nothing but a smooth-talking orphan who had run into trouble with the law. It happened when he tried to impress a slightly older woman at a party by pretending to be an Oxford graduate. Everything went smoothly between them until she introduced him to her brother, a real Oxford scholar who asked detailed questions about the university that he couldn't answer. He hadn't expected any legal consequences from his deception, but it turned out that the brother had a relative at the party who was a police superintendant. Said relative decided to teach him a lesson by means of several days in jail.

After traveling nearly two hours, first on wide carriageways and then on narrow byways, the driver turned the Jaguar into a long tree-lined private lane as the sun began to set. When they emerged from the trees, he saw that the car was approaching an imposing country house of traditional design and obvious age. They followed a circular drive to the massive front entrance and parked. The chauffeur opened the rear door and escorted him to the building entry, where a butler awaited them. Then the driver departed. He was uncertain about what awaited him inside the building, but was determined to carry off this encounter as though he really were someone of substance.

DEPARTURE

(Excerpt from *Impending*)

Cyrus Danforth looked at his image in the mirror and wondered what he had gotten himself into. Here he stood, a hard goods store clerk from Fox Lake, Wisconsin, discharged from the Union Army after Gettysburg with a wooden replacement for his lower left leg, and he had been chosen to pursue a major quest that only started with a journey to Australia. He had never been out of Wisconsin before he joined the Army, and he had only a rough idea of what he would face on his trip to the other side of the world and back. At least Lt. Col. Stevens had given him a promissory note for the cost of his passage plus expenses, which Stevens' brother Charlie had funded. Cyrus knew that George Stevens had not wanted Charlie to know the purpose of his mission, but surprisingly, Charlie had asked no questions while supplying the funds. Danforth supposed his ready compliance to have been due to a combination of wanting to grant his late brother's dying wish and his military training to follow orders.

Cyrus knew that it would take time for the stump from his amputated lower leg to fully heal and for him to get completely acclimated to his wooden replacement, so he had deferred his journey until after the conclusion of the war. Now, in June of 1865, he knew that he had to take action on his adventure. He would follow the plan and trust that God would smile upon his endeavor.

The journey would begin in an hour with his friend and former comrade in arms, Edwin Cole taking him by wagon to the town of Prairie du Chien on the Mississippi River.

As the horse plodded along the road through the tall pine trees, Edwin displayed a big smile. "You single guys get to enjoy adventures while the rest of us have to stay home and raise our kids and crops. I envy you, but I'm satisfied with what I have. You'll probably get rich in that gold rush they have there. That's why you're going, isn't it?"

"You have me pegged right, Ed. I'm going to find out whether I'm lucky or not. I already feel fortunate to have gotten through Gettysburg with only half a leg lost. Poor George Stevens and a whole bunch of our other friends lost their lives there."

"In that sense, I'm fortunate too. I was wounded and discharged at the end of 1862, so that I was already a civilian when all hell broke loose at Gettysburg."

They emerged from the woods and slowed their pace as the road curved its way downhill toward Prairie du Chien and the river. Edwin wanted to be sure that his horse wouldn't stumble while descending the hill. After delivering Cyrus Danforth to the riverfront, he planned to stay overnight to enjoy whatever the town had to offer before returning to his wife and his tedious work routine.

When they approached the steamer dock, both men were surprised by the size of the crowd and the amount of activity they saw. The end of the war had brought the reopening of the southern portion of the Mississippi

River, so that people and goods could once again travel by river to southern cities and the Mississippi Delta. It had been only a month since the surrender at Appomattox Court House, but already the number of Union military uniforms in the crowd had dwindled. This throng was primarily civilian and concerned with personal and business matters.

CAT'S CLAW

(Chapter 1 from *Impasse*)

The big yellow Cat clawed into the earth and scratched up major trouble.

Jerry Krizda nudged the lever on his massive Caterpillar backhoe to force the toothed bucket downward through the stubborn clay and building rubble. The hard obstacle resisted intrusion and then collapsed under the relentless pressure. Jerry rotated the bucket to capture its contents. Then he raised and swiveled the arm to deposit the retrieved conglomeration onto the growing pile alongside the trench. He reached for the lever to rotate the arm back to its digging position, but stopped as his gaze scanned the large pile of debris. His training had prepared him for this eventuality, but he never considered it to be a likely outcome. He sounded the big machine's horn long and loud. Then he waited three seconds and sounded it again. Everyone else on the job stopped what they were doing and came running toward him.

The boss, Ron Barabee, was the first to reach him. "What's the emergency?"

"Look at the top of my pile. We have to stop the job."

Protruding from the hill of debris were three long bones and a human skull. Ron Barabee knew that Krizda was right. The contract documents included American Institute of Architects A201-2007 – General Conditions of the Contract for Construction. Among many other provisions, that document required the contractor to *immediately suspend the operation upon the discovery of human remains or other archaeological findings.* He would have to stop work, contact the police department, and examine the insurance policy covering this job to see whether they honored claims for forced work stoppages. Excavating the site of a strip mall of stores torn down years before should be simple, not bizarre.

Ron Barabee hoped that the bones would turn out to be relatively few and of recent demise. A simple murder or murders would involve only the police. If the forensic pathologist decided the bones were old, the construction delay would be much longer. Archaeologists would have to evaluate the significance of the remains and their appropriate relocation. Those academics could even turn his worksite into an archaeological dig, inaccessible for months or years. Per Ron's instructions, Chuck had already called the police. The piercing throbs of sirens in the distance changed tone as they got closer. This had turned into Barabee's worst work morning in a very long time.

SKY DIVE

(Chapter one from *Stoppers: Aliens in Hallywalooly*)

Malcolm (Mac) Blackwell viewed the patchwork Florida landscape and the distant horizon from the open door of the skydiving plane. He had seen this vista from 10,000 feet before, seven times, the first two as he prepared for tandem jumps harnessed to an instructor, and the last five preceding jumps when he and an instructor descended as a pair of individuals. This was the big one, number eight, his first solo jump. Mac would be the last jumper to leave the aircraft. He was as ready as he could be; an analog altimeter on his wrist and a backup audible altimeter, a Dytter, tucked into his helmet. He had originally set the Dytter to emit beeps at his intended chute-opening altitude of 3,000 feet, but at the last minute he had reset it to 3,500 feet for more time in case the beautiful view caused him to lose focus and ignore his wrist device.

From a point behind his right shoulder, Mac heard his instructor, Roy Ryan yell, "Time!"

Mac grasped both edges of the open doorway and launched himself forward, thinking, but not shouting the traditional *Geronimo* exclamation. As he parted from the aircraft he thought he heard Ryan yell, "Watch your body position!"

The freefall was exhilarating. Mac spread his arms

and legs to add extra area to his body for flight control and scanned the ground beneath him while he tried to tune out the wind noise. It was a beautiful afternoon, but he knew his jump would be the last today for this skydiving company, because a front was due to pass through the area soon.

What was that noise? OhmyGod! It's Dytter time already, 3500 feet from the ground. His wrist altimeter arrow was entering the yellow section, 3,000 feet. He pulled the chute release.

The colorful rectangular canopy billowed above Mac, but he instantly realized all was not well. *Ryan said I needed to watch my body position, and I ignored that. My head was too low, and my shoulders weren't level. I wasn't symmetrical, and now the chute lines are twisted.*

Mac tried to check his wrist altimeter, but the twisted lines had him spinning in circles beneath the canopy. He could see he was in the red danger zone, but he couldn't read numbers. He didn't think he had time to cut the main chute free and open his reserve chute, so he tried something he had read in a skydiving magazine. Mac brought the risers together, squeezed them, and rotated them in the direction opposite to his spin rotation. His spin slowed and gradually stopped. Success. Then he felt a jerk, and looked up at his canopy. More problems.

At lower altitude, Mac had dropped into turbulent air from the oncoming front. The canopy partially collapsed, and he drifted off-course toward some woods and wetlands. He pulled on every line he thought might help, but he had only minor influence on his drift direction.

Mac's thinking raced, and everything seemed to slow down. As a kid, he repeatedly experienced bad dreams in which he died in a car driven over a cliff. This was pretty much the same thing. He wondered what his family would think. They had warned him his skydiving could end up with him dying in a horrible accident. Now they'd be able to say, "I told you so" even though he wouldn't be around to hear it. He might as well go out with as much style and as little damage as possible.

He pulled a riser to aim as best he could for a swamp. The shallow water would cushion his impact a little bit. The canopy was spilling more air, and it was starting to rain. His descent accelerated. His feet hit the water and pushed into the thick vegetation at the bottom of the swamp.

Then, amazingly, the vegetation pushed aside, and Mac continued to fall into an open space beneath the swamp. He hit something soft when he landed, and he had clean air to breathe.

As he came to rest, Mac yelled, "I'm alive! Hallelujah!"

A voice nearby answered, "Not Hallelujah. You're in Hallywalooly."

SPONTANEOUS
TEAMS

(Excerpt from *DECISION TIME! Better Decisions for a Better Life*)

By contrast with the military model, teams tend to work well together without much structure during relief efforts in the aftermath of a disaster. On an overall coordination level, organization and planning are extremely important. This is especially true for massive disasters like the Asian tsunami on December 26, 2004 or Hurricane Katrina in August of 2005. However, on a local level response to a disaster tends to be spontaneous, and people who may have lived alongside each other without communicating suddenly become members of a team. As one example, I was visiting someone near the Massachusetts seacoast during a hurricane some years ago, and when we went outside as the storm eased, we discovered that two cars were floating offshore in the Atlantic Ocean. Very quickly and without organizational direction, people converged at the scene, many of them bringing ropes and cables from their cars and homes. Within just a few minutes we had attached ropes to the floating cars and together with a working group of close to fifty people we were pulling them out of the ocean. This large group of people had become a team spontaneously.

They worked together very efficiently, but after the two floating cars had been retrieved the group dispersed and returned to their various homes. Fortunately, there had not been any people inside those cars. This incident was an isolated one, but similar spontaneous groups arise in cases like sandbagging against rising floodwaters and searching for missing persons. In many disaster situations diverse groups of people converge to work together on a strictly voluntary and mutual assistance basis without any decision-making hierarchy. Many times in such a context someone has said that it takes a disaster to bring us all together.

TELEPHONES

(Excerpt from *After the Storm*, memoir)

I mentioned earlier that we had a party line telephone at home. We had to listen for a dial tone before calling anyone. Sometimes, an unknown person would be talking when we picked up the phone, and then we'd have to quietly put it back down on its hook so that we wouldn't interrupt the other party's conversation. I never found out who our other party was or where they lived. I'm not even sure whether we had only one other party or perhaps more.

Another major aspect of using the telephone was long-distance calling. All long distance calls were multiple-dollar transactions, but you could save money by calling station-to-station where you would speak with anyone who answered the phone, rather than person-to-person where you would be charged a higher amount for only speaking to a specific person. You could also save by calling in the evening rather than during the day.

Regardless of which way you connected, long-distance calling was a major event. Typically, you would gather a large group of family members and/or friends, and each one would take a turn talking to the far-away person within the single long-distance call.

My use of long-distance calling usually involved the facts that we lived in Massachusetts while Dad lived in Florida or my summer excursions to camps. We all learned tricks to save money on telephone calls without exactly cheating.

If I wanted a parent to know I had arrived somewhere safely, I'd call Mom or Dad person-to-person and ask to speak with myself. Naturally, they'd tell the operator I wasn't there, so I'd cancel the call, and there would be no charge, but they had the free message that I had accomplished my mission safely. If I wanted to let Dad know when I would be arriving, I'd call him person-to-person, ask for myself, and during the few seconds when the operator was live on the line, determining that I wasn't with Dad, I'd ask something like, "Will he be there by 5:30 PM?" Dad would say he wasn't sure, and I'd cancel the call, having passed along the information about my 5:30 PM arrival time without a telephone charge. Another version of the *arrived safely* no-cost long distance call would be to call station-to-station on a collect basis. This would require the called party to pay for the call. In this case, the operator would ask the called party whether they would accept a collect call from me. They would decline, hence no cost, but would know that I had called after arriving safely.

Once the government broke up the Bell System telephone monopoly, the separate remaining companies solved the free long-distance calling phenomenon by eliminating operators and changing their rate system to charge for unlimited calling rather than individual calls.

TWO OLD FRIENDS

(Chapter one from the unfinished novel, *Murder Is Dead*)

The scene is a dark-paneled traditional London club. Massive leather-upholstered furniture predominates. In a particularly dim corner of the large room, two old friends take each other's measure.

"I observe that you are a bit bewildered and overly concerned with that newspaper you threw into the fireplace. Old age has not treated you well, Agatha."

"Don't sympathize with my old age, Sherlock. I'm considerably younger than you would be, were you not a fictional character. Even Conan Doyle grew bored with your repetitious ways and wanted to kill you off. Nevertheless, your sensitivity to details remains sharp. I'll grant you that."

"Now, Aggie, let's not nitpick over our relative ages. I have the distinct advantage as what you call a fictional character, that I will never grow old, except for temporary aging within a few of the later novels by Doyle and a variety of imitators."

"Speaking of novels, you do realize that the few novels within your so-called canon, hardly count as such by modern standards. They were too short to qualify. No twenty-first century publisher would accept them as novels."

"Ah, there's the rub. You don't like the twenty-first

century. What would you have us do to change it? We are, Dear Lady, loosed of the confines of time at this point, and we are free to operate anywhere and anytime as well."

"We were from the golden age, Sherlock. People cared about their murders then, particularly because they were rare events. This modern world with its perpetual street gunfire and random violence is no friend to mystery authors. Season that deadly stew with international terrorism, and you have little room for the skillfully planned and solved individual murder. Mystery authors have become anticlimax shadows of their former selves."

"So, the large-screen dynamic world has interfered with your country mansion high-society values. You've become a pessimist, Agatha. I, Sherlock Holmes, will show you the errors in your evaluation of the new large-scale violence. Perhaps we will even contribute to its diminishment."

A smartly-attired balding man with a perfectly groomed mustache rises from a nearby chair where his presence has been concealed by that seat's high backrest. "Quite right, Holmes, we should relieve Agatha's apprehensions, but we do not have to do so by infiltrating gangs and terrorism groups. We should simply use the little gray cells that God and our authors have given us."

1776

(Chapter one from *Loyalties: Uncertain / Mixed / Fanatical*)

Martin Weatherford heard a thump at his front door as he was preparing to go upstairs to bed. The enslaved house servants had retired to their small rooms over the kitchen, so Martin went to the door himself. When he opened it, he found his son John sitting on the top step, examining an unopened bottle of whiskey.

"You've had enough to drink, John. Come inside and go to bed."

"I don't think you realize how significant this bottle is, Father. I received it as a bonus when I signed up for the Continental Army. You may still consider yourself a subject of the King, but I've chosen to be a free American."

"You're out of your mind. You spend too much time at the tavern with those rabble rousers. There will be no country of America, just the thirteen colonies. The British Army will put down the rebellion within months. You and your upstart band of commoner friends will end up dead or in prison. Sober up and realize how fortunate we are to have ample property protected by British law. Your brothers and your sister aren't talking rebellion foolishness. They know how to appreciate our land holdings and our place in colonial Georgia society. New Englanders and Pennsylvanians are the main ones preaching separation from England. It's the impossible dream of poor tradesmen and farmers. It will never happen. Be reasonable, John."

"I can't agree with you, Father. People came here from England and other countries to get away from class systems that limited their potential. You like the King because you've done well under his rule, but I'll cast my lot with the majority of people over here who want to live free and succeed based on their skills, not their class position in society. I'll be leaving to join the Continental Army tomorrow. There are scholars and politicians working right now in Philadelphia on a Declaration of Independence from England. I'll be supporting them from the start."

"You'll be living on scraps like the rest of your rabble friends. If you leave this house, you won't be welcomed back. I'll disown you and remove you from my will. How well will you cope with poverty?"

"If that's your attitude, I'll pack a few things and leave tonight. Goodbye, Father. This war may not treat you as well as you think it will."

HURRICANE DORIAN'S AFTERMATH

(Excerpt from the unfinished novel, *Imperiled*)

On the day following Hurricane Dorian's lingering move northwest of Great Abaco, after his wife, Judy, and grandson, John Sandy Weatherford caught their Bahamas air flight out of the small Treasure Cay Airport, north of Marsh Harbour, George Weatherford gathered some first aid supplies at the hospital and headed toward the Weatherford & Rolle building materials store on foot. He gave thanks for his sturdy boots as he followed flooded roads surrounded on both sides by shreds of houses, scattered vehicles ranging from motorbikes to ocean-going cargo containers, and pieces of broken trees. George found many of the roads passable on foot, even though he occasionally had to wade through the surrounding mud and floodwaters in spots where debris completely blocked the way. Slightly unfamiliar odors would soon ripen into the stench of death when searchers arrived to probe the wreckage for missing persons. As he trudged along, dodging obstacles, George heard nothing but an occasional barking dog and the wind. The hurricane was gone, leaving bright sunshine in its wake, but stiff breezes continued, frequently slowing George's progress when they shifted to blow into his face. At least the island was tropical and the temperature remained mild. His thoughts were interrupted by a loud chopping sound behind him. George stopped and turned his head to see a U.S. Coast Guard helicopter flying overhead. He strode forward again, waving to signal them that he was all right. A crewman sitting in the open cabin doorway waved his acknowledgment as the helicopter banked and turned toward Marsh Harbour's damaged and flooded Leonard M. Thompson International Airport. George began to tire as he trudged along, realizing that his detours to avoid debris and flooding were doubling the length of his hike to the store.

As he moved off the road to avoid a particularly large pile of rubble from several destroyed buildings, George stopped and stiffened in horror. Protruding from beneath the wreckage were two sets of legs, one belonging to a woman and one to a child. They were pinned beneath pieces of concrete that were too heavy for him to lift. He wished that he had discovered these bodies before encountering the Coast Guard helicopter, but that source of assistance was gone. The best he could do was to find a long narrow sliver of a board, push it into the ground near the bodies, and tie a shred of cloth to it to serve as a marker for search and rescue teams to see later.

When George finally reached the driveway leading to the Weatherford & Rolle building, he paused to evaluate the scene he faced.

The parking lot of the store was filled with tree and shrub branches. It was paved, but in the few places that weren't obscured by other debris, the surface was covered with chunks of concrete and cinder blocks from nearby buildings that had been partially or totally destroyed. The only patches of color were cars that were unlikely to ever drive again. One silver car had its hood completely torn off, revealing an engine compartment filled with sand and twigs. The car's roof was dented above the driver's seat as were its door panels. All of its window glass was missing, suggesting that this car had rolled over several times during the hurricane. A blue car with its driver's door open was intact but filled with rubbish, having been saved from a rollover only because it was wedged between the front of the building and a doorless horizontal freezer. An upside down red car was barely visible beneath wind-blown tree trunks and branches.

The Weatherford & Rolle building no longer bore its impressive sign. That insignia had disappeared, along with the roof of the entry and front office sections of the store. The walls and roof of the main sales area were intact, but the roof was stripped of shingles, and very little of the underlying tar paper remained. The concrete block wall that surrounded the loading dock side of the building was rubble except for a strong corner section that remained standing. No glass remained in any of the store windows.

George climbed over piles of brush and picked his way through other obstacles on his way to the building. When he was halfway across the parking lot, he thought he saw someone waving through a glassless window. He responded by waving his arm above his head. Then he squinted to see better and discovered the waving person was only a shred of white cloth moving in the breeze.

LAUGH AND LOSE WEIGHT

(Three verses from *Slimmericks* without their illustrations)

The exercise bug must have bit me.
I feel guilty whenever I sit me.
I balance and stretch
'til I want to retch,
But my very old trousers still fit me.

Your snacks are the devil's delight.
He wants you to eat them all night.
Just close up that box
And be a smart fox
That keeps moving and makes muscles tight.

If you want to lose lots of weight
Eat only foods that you hate.
You'll eat very few
For a much slimmer you
And you'll end up feeling just great.

ABOUT THE AUTHOR

Richard Davidson is the author of the self-help guidebook, *DECISION TIME!* He has written the five-novel Lord's Prayer Mystery Series, the six-novel Imp Mystery Series, *Slimmericks*, a childhood memoir: *After the Storm*, the six-course Lenten Bible Study Series: *Email Jesus*, and a science-fiction novel: *Stoppers*. He has also edited an anthology: *Overcoming*. He is an aeronautical & astronautical engineer.

BOOKS BY THIS AUTHOR

Decision Time!

Overcoming

Slimmericks

Lead Us Not Into Temptation

Give Us This Day Our Daily Bread

Forgive Us Our Trespasses

Thy Will Be Done

Deliver Us From Evil

Implications

Impulses

Impostor

Impending

Impasse

Loyalties

Email Jesus, Course 1

Email Jesus Course 2

Email Jesus Course 3

After The Storm

Stoppers